Saeed Al-Ali is an Emirati author, who wrote cartoons for TV; *Blood In The Sand* is his first book, and his first project aimed to a mature audience that talks about a more serious subject, Saeed wishes to turn his book to an animated series one day.

Ethan Hunter is an American academy winning screenwriter, who wrote for TV series, sitcoms, movies. Most of his writings got produced and won awards. *Blood In The Sand* is his first novel co-written with Saeed Al-Ali.

Both authors come from different backgrounds and together they handcrafted the story of *Blood In The Sand*, which is an English novel based in future Dubai.

I would like to dedicate this book to:

My father, who is also my hero.

My Mother, an angel in human form.

And finally my wife and kids, who are the sources of my strength.

Saeed Al-Ali and Ethan Hunter

BLOOD IN THE SAND

AUSTIN MACAULEY PUBLISHERS™

LONDON * CAMBRIDGE * NEW YORK * SHARJAH

Copyright © Saeed Al-Ali and Ethan Hunter 2023

The right of Saeed Al-Ali and Ethan Hunter to be identified as author of this work has been asserted by the author in accordance with sections 77 and 78 of the Copyright, Designs and Patents Act 1988.

All rights reserved. No part of this publication may be reproduced, stored in a retrieval system, or transmitted in any form or by any means, electronic, mechanical, photocopying, recording, or otherwise, without the prior permission of the publishers.

Any person who commits any unauthorised act in relation to this publication may be liable to criminal prosecution and civil claims for damages.

This is a work of fiction. Names, characters, businesses, places, events, locales, and incidents are either the products of the author's imagination or used in a fictitious manner. Any resemblance to actual persons, living or dead, or actual events is purely coincidental.

A CIP catalogue record for this title is available from the British Library.

ISBN 9781035820108 (Paperback)
ISBN 9781035820115 (Hardback)
ISBN 9781035820139 (ePub e-book)

www.austinmacauley.com

First Published 2023
Austin Macauley Publishers Ltd®
1 Canada Square
Canary Wharf
London
E14 5AA

I would like to acknowledge the land of opportunities Dubai, where anything is possible!

Prologue

She runs. She thinks it will help. We slither after her, winding toward her. Undeniable.

She stomps. She screams. We are silent. We are inevitable.

We hunt.

We smell her fear and will not be lost.

She turns down a hallway. Gasps. Sobs. There is no escape. There is only us, now.

She pounds and scratches and claws for freedom. Her nails tear from her white flesh. Her fingers cry crimson tears.

She begins to think hope is lost. She is incorrect. We are hope.

We are a promise. We must be fulfilled.

Her freckled face and blond hair are wet and tiger-striped with running mascara. She wails and begs.

She does not understand.

She is a single cell of the old skin. One part of the dying husk that must be shed so we can be reborn. So we can transform. So we can heal. So we may reach for and find immortality.

She should rejoice. They never rejoice.

Her sacrifice will not be forgotten.

She shouts for help until her voice cracks and breaks. It will not come.

There is nowhere left to run. Nowhere to hide. There is only this now. The slow and terrible path to salvation.

We are coiled. We strike.

Our steel fangs are sharp. So sharp she doesn't feel the punctures. Our venom works fast. She is paralyzed instantly.

She is quiet now.

She leaks.

Her life pools before her and is gathered by our hands and lips and tongues.

She is still alive when we begin to feed. When we open her and find the pieces we require. When we take what we need from inside.

She is not the beginning. Not the end. Only one of hundreds of thousands who must be shed according to the ancient ways. So that we may rise.

Someday, there will only be us. There will only be serpents, and their holy serpent queen.

Until then, we hunt.

Chapter 1

I pick up one of the eleven envelopes in my passenger seat stamped with "FINAL NOTICE," in big red letters, set it on fire, and use it to light my eightieth cigarette of the day.

Those bills used to terrify me. I used to dread them like you dread seeing a dentist that's sleeping with your wife. Now I think of them like seasoning for the tobacco. Like adding a dash of saffron to rice, lighting a Silk Cut with a bill you can't pay is an acquired taste that can elevate the entire experience. All the best things in life really do live on the other side of fear.

My phone hates me. She alerts me too late that my exit is coming up. So I change lanes a little too fast on the E 11 and something falls off the car. Instinctively I spend a few seconds hoping it wasn't something important before reason takes the wheel and I remember I don't care. I am not remotely bothered by this or really anything. Nobody ever tells you how freeing well and truly giving up is.

Today there are many millions of cars here in Dubai. In 1968, the year my father was born, there were only 13 cars registered in this entire city, and this thing I'm willing down the highway is so old it just may have been one of them.

It's not only ancient, it's trash. It's held together by more duct tape and hope than steel. It looks and smells like something that died in the sun a long time ago. It's worth less than the paper the bills for it are printed on. I triple its value every time I fill up the leaky tank. But they still tried to repossess it last week. Joke was on them, though. They couldn't repo it 'cause the city had already booted it for all the parking tickets I also can't pay.

I was a cop a few years back though. In another life. And I know that if you've got a flathead screwdriver and an adjustable seven-millimetre tubular lock pick, boots can fall away from tires as easy as your old friends when they see you on the other side of the holding cell bars for the first time. Sounds like some fancy spy gear or something, right? An adjustable tubular lock pick. You can get a set of three on Amazon for twenty bucks. With free two-day delivery. Welcome to the future. Everything sucks.

I half expect this car to just explode on me whenever I turn over the circa 1620 ignition and I'm not gonna lie, for just a moment, before I remember I don't care, a little part of me is pretty disappointed every time that doesn't happen. I used to drive a Bugatti. I'm way more embarrassed by the Bugatti.

The phone rings and I see it's my brother calling. He's got another conspiracy theory for me, or he wants to call in one of the sixty thousand favours I owe him. I silence the phone and promise myself I'll get back to him as soon as the case is done.

Just as I'm about to light smoke number eighty-one I drive right past the place I'm going and a few seconds later my phone tells me I reached my destination. I whip around and look for somewhere out of the way to park. This should be good and weird at least.

I've been hired by a very angry woman, that's nothing new. She thinks her man is doing her wrong. She wants pictures that invalidate the prenup. She's gonna take him for all he's worth. That's all standard, boilerplate stuff for a dick like me. Whatever the hell a boilerplate is. Where it gets a little interesting is the guy who done this lady wrong, it's his birthday. He just turned 94.

Viagra is one hell of a drug. Science leads the way.

It's actually my birthday, too. I just turned 30. I say a little prayer that I die before I get as old and lame as the dude whose endless life I'm about to ruin.

I park six blocks away and try to get a sense of just how many poor choices I'm about to make. If past is prologue, a lot.

My target lives in a luxury retirement community. Of course, he does. It's Dubai. Everything here is either super luxurious or it's on fire. This one is called 'Enduring Light.' From the outside it looks like the American White House, only nicer and with a pool and more palm trees. The security is about as tight, too.

There's a twelve-foot concrete wall surrounding the compound and two armed guards patrolling the only gate leading into grounds. You gotta wonder if they're trying to keep people out or if they're trying to keep these poor old geezers in.

Almond trees line a lot of the wall outside. Should be a breeze to scale one to get inside the complex. But like all prisons, getting in isn't the hard part.

Before I head on in I grab the green duffle bag from my trunk. This is my crybaby tonight. What's a crybaby, you ask? It's an invention of my own design. Never leave home without it.

I approach the wall as silently as possible. I control my breathing. I stick to the shadows and move from cover to cover with one eye on the guards the whole time. They never look up from the video games they're playing on their phones. Yeah, I'm thinking the idea is definitely to keep people in.

A couple of quick steps on a couple of thick branches and I'm up and over the wall. I stow the crybaby in a dark corner and head toward the apartment my client said would be ground zero. It's dark out here and bright inside, nearly impossible for any of the folk in the building to see me. But I can see them. They're watching soap operas in one room, having after-dinner coffees and sweets in another. In a gym, some of them walk as briskly as their 200-year-old legs can carry them atop treadmills that definitely cost more than my pitiful car.

Then I make it to the outside of room 107, just on the eastern corner of the building. And the angry woman was right. They almost always are. Inside is her husband and some lady who is definitely not his wife. And what they are doing will haunt my nightmares until the end of my days, I'm certain. It's sex. Sure. I guess. Technically. But it's a horror show version. Like someone shaved two arthritic pugs and forced them to play history's most disturbing game of Twister.

I could resell these photos to abstinence-only programs across the globe. It'd put kids off sex forever. Hell, these images could make people hate the idea of sex so hard no children are ever born again. With what I'm documenting here tonight, I could end the human race. It's that gross. Nobody would miss us.

But I'm not here to judge. Or to destroy humanity. I'm here to end a marriage. I'm here to take photos. So I do. I pop the cap off my Canon 7D, point, and shoot.

I take snap after snap after snap of content so dang disturbing I know I'll have flashbacks every time I eat a bagel that someone left in the boiler just a little too long.

This is a terrible gig. It's not glamorous. It's maybe not even honorable. But when I asked the angry woman what she'd pay me to do this she said, "Very little." And I'm in no position to turn down an offer like that. And if you don't want to get caught cheating on your wife of sixty years, maybe don't cheat on your wife of sixty years.

So I watch. And I take my terrible photos.

His stamina is pretty good, I gotta say. Maybe I should try Pilates or water aerobics or whatever this guy is into. It goes on for a while. When I think it can't get worse he jerks his head back in pleasure and his teeth fly out mid-climax. They land several feet away.

The lady spits her teeth into her hand and hurls them across the room in I guess solidarity. That's pretty sweet actually. Maybe these two will make it work when he's divorced and penniless. Maybe. Assuming she's loaded.

He worked his whole life, probably. Built things or bought and sold and traded things. Served people he hated, probably. He pulled himself up by his bootstraps, maybe. Burnt the candle at both ends to get ahead in the fastest growing city in history. Made the kind of money you need to have made to retire in a bonkers resort like this. And he's throwing it all away as casually as that lady threw out her teeth just for a moment of feeling wanted again. My goodness, we're a stupid species. How we made it this far is beyond me.

No way we make it another century. No way.

I know I've got the shots. Enough to get paid. Enough for my client to take her husband to the cleaners six times over. But I want some close-ups. I inch forward. I get greedy. I get too close. I trigger about a hundred million watts of motion-activated security floodlights. I'm lit up like a prima ballerina on center stage.

The old guy spins and looks right at me.

I freeze like maybe he's a T-Rex and his vision is based on movement or something and if I stay still enough I'll be invisible. But he's not a T-Rex. And I'm very much visible. He sees me. And he heads right for the window.

Like an idiot, I stay frozen. He's a thousand years old. He's naked. He doesn't have his teeth. There's no way he's climbing out a window in the middle of the night to come after me.

He climbs out a window in the middle of the night to come after me.

He sprints right for me and he's spry, man. Deceptively quick. This guy was an athlete in his youth. Or a dang cheetah or something. And, how do I put this delicately? The little blue pills are still doing their job. Viagra is a helluva drug.

The whole thing is so funny I forget to move until he's nearly on top of me.

Finally, my slack, threadbare wits return to me and I spin on my heel and I run. If you want to make it as a private detective, running away is the single most important skill you'll need to master. I know I can't make it over that wall, though, and the guards are still at the gate. And they've still got guns. I'm boxed in.

This is why I always pack a crybaby.

A crybaby is just a device that makes a lot of noise and light. There's no specific recipe because I build them mostly out of stuff I find in dumpsters. It's anything that will command a whole heck of a lot of attention in a hurry. I got the idea from an old TV show I watched when I was a kid.

The one I brought tonight is an old car alarm, half a packet of bottle rockets, and an expired road flare. I've rigged the whole thing to a pink Hello Kity burner phone I found in a puddle outside a preschool and set everything to go off when it gets a text.

I take my own phone from my pocket and yell into it as I run. "Hey, Siri. Text Hello Kitty."

"What would you like the text to say?" my phone asks me.

"Crybaby cry. Make your mamma sigh."

My phone says, "Text sent."

And somewhere behind me, my green duffel bag starts screaming and exploding and catching fire.

It's the first time the guards have looked up from their phones all night. They hasten toward the flames. If they even notice me and the naked nonagenarian chasing me, they don't show it. They just need to stop the noise and put out the fire. The crybaby does its job yet again.

As they zip past me they're yelling in Arabic. They're blaming each other for losing the fire extinguisher. I try so hard not to laugh.

I've got a decent lead on the naked fossil hot on my heels as I bolt through the iron gates of Enduring Light Luxury Retirement Community. About a block later I slow to a jog and then to a walk. And I'm still laughing.

My life is garbage, sure, but there's joy to be found in some things.

I'm about four blocks from my car when I hear something behind me. Something like a whine or a whizzing. And it's getting louder. It's getting closer. I turn to see what's happening and it turns out the old naked maniac has found himself a golf cart. Not just any golf cart, some kind of souped-up, supercharged thing. He's closing fast. And he's waving what looks like a machete that he got I-don't-know-where.

Legs churning, lungs burning, I race back toward my old beater. He's closing fast and I'm starting to wonder who wins a fight between me, a run-down detective who smokes too much, or the angriest naked retiree in the world with a giant knife.

I'm half a block from the car when I see the last bit of great news in my charmed life. Bright yellow steel, round and mocking me and stuck right to my bald tires. Those pricks booted my car again! It's not going anywhere right now.

New plan.

The United Arab Emirates has only existed since 1971. And one of the huge advantages of growing up in a country younger than my parents is I know my way around. When I was a kid fifty, maybe sixty percent of what you see in Dubai today in 2025, didn't exist yet. This place was dreamed into existence in the blink of a cosmic eye. I know the roads and I know the shortcuts because I was here when they built them. So I get my bearings. We're not far from the old commercial district.

I check my watch. This time of night on a Friday, there are always kushti matches going on down there. There will be a couple of hundred people watching. I can get lost in the crowd.

I take a hard right just as my nude predator takes a swing with his machete. He's so close I can feel the wind off the blade as it whips past my shoulder. I'm not laughing anymore.

Fast as the little cart is, though, it can't corner for beans. My guy giving chase has to make a wide arc and come back around. It's enough time to put a little more distance between us.

I make it to the fish market and the matches are in full effect like always. The crowd goes wild as one of the wrestlers is almost pinned to the sand but breaks free. I weave between bodies. I hunch my shoulders. Stay low. Work around the perimeter of the match.

I hear people gasp. I hear a few shrieks. I hear swearing in at least six different languages. That's not for the wrestlers. That's the sound of a lot of people meeting a very angry, very naked grandad. And suddenly it's all pretty funny again.

I chance a look back and my nude friend is being escorted away by some volunteer security guards. He's been relieved of his machete. I'm home free. My stupid night is finally done. For once, I win. Suck it, world.

And then my phone dings.

I check the text message. It's from an unknown number. It says, "Khalifa, I'm so sorry. Your brother is dead."

Chapter 2

I don't have siblings. Not by blood. But I have a brother. Had a brother. I guess.

A brother in law in my twenties, and a brother in arms before that, but long before either, a brother by that much stronger bond boys can only form at a certain age. We were joined by a chain made of endless summers and unfettered joy and hope and possibility spread in front of two people more immense and sweeping than deserts and dreams. A brotherhood of broken bones and promises kept.

If someone took him from me a whole lot of people should prepare to die. I'm gonna make the lawyers and undertakers of this city rich.

I check all of the news sites and gossip blogs. Flip through Twitter, Facebook, Snapchat, Tick Tock, Instagram, and every other terrible vanity app I can think of. There's no mention of Humaid's death anywhere. He was rich enough and connected enough that his demise would definitely be talked about in most places at least a little. But nothing.

That tells me either the person who sent me the message is a cop on the scene with early, first-hand knowledge, or somebody is messing with me. Enough people hate me these days that I find the last drop of hope left in my ridiculous body and hold onto it. Maybe it's a prank. Maybe it's just another bit of cruelty flung at me. Maybe my brother isn't dead.

Maybe if I'd just answered my phone none of this would be a problem. Why is it we silence the calls we always need to take the most? Some jilted gajillionaire wants to pay me half a Clark bar to take gross pictures and I answer on the second ring. My brother needs me to save his life and I'll get around to it when I get around to it.

A second text message came in not long after the first. It told me if I wanted to learn more I needed to head down to Al Marmoom RaceTrack deep in the desert. Of course, I wanted to know more. Just try to stop me from knowing more.

The people of this city think they took everything from me? I never lost the guns.

I kept my distance as my naked great, great, great grandad was escorted away and then I booked it back to my broken-down ride, my raggedy heart pumping and thumping way harder than when I was being chased by a maniac with a sword a few minutes ago.

It's amazing how often I look back at the terrible awful almost-died stuff I've been through as the good old days.

It takes me about five minutes to get the boot off my car and another forty-five to get to Al Marmoom, the largest camel racing track in Dubai. It should have only taken about thirty minutes at this time of night, but I changed lanes too fast again. This time a tire actually did fall off my car and it took some time to find it and put it back on.

The deep, dark ocean of pulsing blue lights outside the track as I pull up nearly drowns me. The bends I get trying to surface rip my stomach into a hundred shreds. There are 17,500 men and women on the Dubai Police Force and I swear every single one of them must be here right now.

Whoever texted me wasn't messing with me. Somebody important died here tonight. He's gone. I want to scream and I want to hurt things but more than that I need to be as professional as I can still manage. At least for a little while. I need to find the person or the people who did this and I need them to die slow. It's important to have goals in life.

I'm not egotistical enough to think Humaid's death has anything to do with me. Even with the nonstop crap storm that is my life, I'm not far-gone enough to think the universe hates me. Because the truth is obvious and much more terrifying: the universe doesn't give a single crap about any of us. It is utterly indifferent. And even if it weren't, I'm just not that important.

I know this isn't about me, but as I step out of what's left of my car, I can't help but wonder a little. Places like this are where he and I became inseparable when we were kids. When we were maybe five years old or so. We started here. He ended here. Maybe this is what finally gets me, too. I'm fine with it, but not before I shove my boot up enough butts to get to the bottom of this. Not before at least one more body drops.

Why the camel races?

Why the desert?

Up until 2002, it didn't occur to anyone here that using children as the jockeys in Camel racing was super messed up I guess. Children, babies practically, strapped onto a 500-kilogram monster screaming down a ten-kilometre track at sixty kph seemed just fine to most folk. At least it seemed fine to anyone who had the power to change it. Seemed fine to me, too, to be honest. It was my first job. I don't know what the hell was wrong with my parents that they let me do that, but I mean to ask them one of these days.

I was an ideal combination of small and strong for my age. And I was fearless. And I was good. Maybe it was the last thing I was good at, who knows?

Humaid's family was rich, rich like you mean it, and he got them to bet on me. I made them a lot of money and they celebrated with me and something rare and good and pure was born: friendship.

Today, they've got freaky little robots they use as jockeys. And the older men in the crowds and on the radios cry about what we've lost as a culture now that the chances of toddlers being crushed to death for sport are slightly lower than they used to be.

But that's tradition for you, I guess.

Camels are all about tradition here in the sand. Before we were a megacity, before we built the tallest building in history and before we made ski resorts inside malls in the dang desert, before the oil and the pearls made us masters of the universe, there were camels. Camels were the ships of the dune sea. Everything relied on them. The trade and spice routes that made my people, the original Emiratis, descendants of nomadic tribes, who we are were not possible without camels. Literally, I and everyone I know is not possible without camels.

And today they run in a circle for money.

That's tradition for you.

I take four seconds to breathe in deeply through my mouth. I hold the air in my lungs for four seconds. I count to four once more as I slowly exhale through my mouth. Box breathing, they call it in the American special forces. It's supposed to center you. Focus you. I learned about it from a movie starring Seth Rogen. Anyway. I breathe. It helps a little. Not enough. And I head for the gate.

I recognize my old cruiser in the parking lot. That means Afra is here. My partner. Former partner. My friend. Maybe not former friend? We'll see if her presence works in my favor or not. Maybe it will. There's a first time for everything, I'm told.

"No!" says a voice I know like I know my own name.

I look up and come face to face with Afra for the first time in months that feel like decades. The face I used to look forward to seeing every single day.

"Khalifa," she says. "What are you even doing here?" "I got a text. Somebody said Humaid is dead. I didn't have a choice, Afra. You get that, right?"

"Who texted you?"

"Unknown. Doesn't matter. Is it true?"

"It matters to me," she says sternly. She's risen in the ranks a couple of times in the eleven months since I got booted off the force and the authority looks good on her. Gotta wonder if I was holding her back. As that thought zips through my wastebasket of a mind I'm surprised to learn I actually do care if I was bad for her. "Is it true," I ask, a little harsher this time. Though it must read as desperation and sadness.

Her face softens into pity and I know it's true. She stops being a cop, at least for a second, and remembers she's my friend. "Come with me," she says, motioning toward the track.

More and more officers part like the red sea to let her pass as she walks me toward the body. She speaks loudly, making sure everyone around us can hear what she's saying. "I'll give you a quick look, you deserve that much, but you cannot investigate this. You hear me? You cannot go near this case. We will handle it."

"If my brother is dead you won't be able to stop me. I'm sorry Afra, really I am. I don't want to jam you up. If this is really Humaid, if he's gone you're just about the only thing left on this awful blue marble I give two craps about. But I can't stand idly by."

"Dang it, Khalifa. I am trying to do you a favor. In my entire life, you're the hardest sack of crap I've ever seen to help. Stay away from this. If you don't I will arrest you and I will hold you until it's over." She turns on her heel and stops me. She looks right into my eyes and she demands, "Stay out of it."

And I want to help her. I would do just about anything for this person. I really would. And I say, "No." And over her shoulder, I can see the body.

I don't need to get too close to know it's him. The deep-set eyes and the aquiline nose are a dead giveaway. Like Alfred Hitchcock, anyone who's ever seen Humaid could identify him from his silhouette alone. My brother is most definitely dead.

But when I'm only a few feet away I see more. What skin is left on him is bruised black and blue. The rest is just shredded meat. His legs are tied at the ankles. He was dragged behind a camel for miles. They did it while he was alive. Dead bodies don't bruise.

When I find whoever did this, I'm going to make this a new tradition.

Then I kneel beside the body and I see just how much trouble I'm in.

His stomach has been ripped open, his guts are on display like a museum piece. I don't need to be a doctor to immediately be certain about what went on in there. "His liver and his gallbladder are gone, yeah?" I ask, already knowing the answer.

"Yes," she says. "Just like…" and she stops herself from finishing that sentence because she knows there's no need.

There's no need, but I finish it for her, "Just like my wife."

Chapter 3

I stand up from the body and something else is dead in me now, too. Funny thing is, I would have sworn there was nothing left alive in there.

There's always more to lose.

Afra is looking at me with desperation in those deep brown eyes. She looks at me like nobody else does. Like there's something worth saving in me. I don't have the heart to correct her. That was burned out of me long ago.

"I'm not going to investigate this," I say.

She just squints at me and tilts her head a little.

Disbelief.

"Really. This person this…thing. He beat me before.

"Beat me like a drum. Broke me down like fractions, Afra. Took everything from me and was cruel enough to leave me alive to boot. I got nothing left to fight him. He wins. I'm done."

And Afra can see that I mean it. That I really am done. And somehow that's worse for her, I think, than if I were still kicking her cops in their balls and tearing up the city looking for answers despite all of her warnings and pleas. There are two great tragedies in life, they say. The first is not getting what you want. And the second is getting it.

I just turn and walk away from all of it. There's junk food and junk TV to watch at my parents' house. If I really go for it, I can get another eighty cigarettes smoked before bed. It's important to have goals.

And that's when Afra's boss's boss's boss walks into my life. "Khalifa bin Ahmed," he says. "You're under arrest for the murder of Humaid Bin Salem."

"Sure," I think. "This might as well happen."

Chapter 4

Here's what you say to the cops: Nothing. Ever. Not one single thing.

If you're under arrest, you say nothing. If you're a suspect, you say nothing. If one passes you on the street and says, "Good afternoon," don't even nod your head at them. Just demand a lawyer and shut up. No good can come of talking to them and all kinds of bad most surely can. We…they, I mean, will twist and turn any statement, any inconsistency, any single word into any shape they please. Like watching a birthday party clown turn one sausage-shaped balloon into a poodle, police can mangle any utterance into confession, into probable cause, into evidence of conspiracy reaching anywhere and everywhere. I know this to be true because I did it for a living.

But it's worse than that. Laws are written to be as vague as possible so that almost anything can be called a crime. And almost anything you say can be turned into an admission of a crime.

"I was just walking to work," you might say.

"On the sidewalk? With those shoes? So you admit to destruction of public property."

I promise you I've seen that one and I've seen dumber. And I've seen them get convictions.

The system is purpose-built to screw you.

So as they put the handcuffs on two clicks too tight, I am silent.

And as they load me into the back of the car making sure to bump my head three separate times, I am quiet as a church mouse.

And as they drive me the long way 'round back to the station, hoping the sheer boredom or confinement will get me to open up, I do not make a peep.

As they sit me down far too hard into the meanspirited metal chair of the interrogation room, I only smile and hand them my lawyer's business card. The cop in here with me, Tahir, I think his name was, tears it up in front of me and tosses it in the air, letting it fall on the brushed steel table like confetti.

I smile into the white plastic camera mounted in the corner and hand him another card. Same result. It's okay. I've got lots of these cards on me. I get arrested pretty often these days.

His partner comes in and I can tell from the jump she's supposed to be the good cop. We've met a few times but I can't remember her name.

"Hey, Khalifa. Welcome back," she says with a grin.

"Always nice to see old friends."

I don't smile. I don't nod. I hand her my lawyer's business card. She doesn't tear it up. She also has no interest in calling my attorney. She has no interest in me having rights. She's the good cop.

I used to be the good cop, too.

None of it matters. I called my lawyer on the way to the racetrack and told him to meet me here if he didn't hear from me in an hour. I always assume any time I'm within a kilometre of police that I will be arrested for something. I'm almost always right.

Tahir gets in my face which I guess is supposed to frighten me. The smell of the kabab he had for dinner on his breath is a little scary, I must admit. Way too much garlic. "Killing your own wife wasn't enough for a sicko like you, huh?" he says. "You had to go back for her brother."

When I continue to sit silently, he slaps the table as hard as he can and then fails miserably to hide the pain he caused himself. I try to stop it but I just can't help myself and for a moment I do smile.

The lady cop asks me something, I don't even pay attention to what it is. I'm not going to answer anyway.

We're near the one-year anniversary of my first time on the wrong side of this table. My wife Hanah was killed on February first of this year. I was questioned, which I didn't take all that personally, to be honest. Forget butlers, the husband almost always did it. And I talked. These were my friends. I told them exactly where I was and what I had been doing. I did this through fits of sobs and tears and grief so thick I choked on it over and over.

To a police with an agenda, crying over your dead wife is a confession.

About six hours into the interrogation I realized my life was fully over. Hanah was gone, my career was gone, and probably my freedom was gone. I was being railroaded.

Some maniac smashed her head with a chunk of black marble, cut her open, and removed her gallbladder and liver. And I was going down for it.

There was no way it was true. My alibi was rock solid, there wasn't one piece of evidence, I had no motive, no history of violence, and these people knew me, liked me I thought. And every single cop still went along with the story like it didn't matter that they were feeding one of their own to the lions. Like it couldn't just as easily be them next. Every cop but Afra. And her I had to beg and fight and threaten to stay away from me so this didn't take her down, too.

I grew up poor as dirt but I married rich. It took every dime Hanah had, every dime I had, and every dime my parents had to fight it and it still wasn't enough. If Humaid hadn't gone against his parents' wishes and pulled strings, I'd still be in prison.

The cops are still talking, I guess. To me, it just sounds like flies buzzing in my ear. Then finally my lawyer arrives. His name is Barry. He's American. He's not very good at his job. But he owes me favours, and favours are all I can afford these days.

He's not even a full-time lawyer. He makes ends meet by selling shoes a couple of times a week. He gives me a pretty good discount on last year's models.

"I'd like to speak with my client alone, please." He says. Nobody moves. He takes out a piece of paper and starts writing. "Then I may as well start working on my lawsuit. I'll be naming you both personally so I hope you like depositions and also losing your homes."

With eye rolls so loud they shake the room, the two officers head out. As they walk away Barry calls to the lady. "And those heels with that top…honey, no."

The young cop looks actually hurt by this and I've never been more proud to have a lawyer that works out of a shopping mall.

"I assume you've said nothing."

"Of course not. Learned that lesson several hard ways."

"And your boots, they're comfortable?"

"Come on, man."

"Fair enough."

"Listen," I say, leaning in close because the walls of course have ears, "if they want to push this, there's definitely security camera footage of me breaking into a nursing home tonight during the time of death window and being chased by a naked dude who was roughly 180 years old."

"Sounds like must-see TV."

"I think you're really going to enjoy it. It's a crime, but it's not murder. Find it and put it online. Shop it to the news stations, too. It's out there enough that it should get some play. Definitely don't turn the only copy over to the police. They will lose it."

"It's not my first rodeo, Khalifa. I'm on it. You need anything else?"

"Just call my folks. I missed my birthday dinner. They'll be worried."

Barry nods and starts gathering up his things when Afra walks in.

"I'm still talking to my client. I'll thank you not to…"

"It's fine," I say. "She's fine."

Barry shrugs. "Suit yourself. I'll get on the thing and have you out in a jiffy."

Barry leaves and Afra sits down across from me. She's shed all the edges and angles she was made of before. She doesn't look like an officer. She looks like my friend.

"You okay?" She asks.

"As ever," I say and even I don't know if I'm telling the truth. Probably not.

"Look, we can talk. The cameras and mics are off—promise."

"What's there to talk about? Obviously, I didn't kill my brother."

"Obviously," she agrees. "But whoever did, whoever is pulling strings in the department and wherever else the strings go, they nearly got you last time and they may want another bite at the apple. Or they may just go ahead and kill you this time like they did with Humaid. I know I told you not to look into this back at the track, but that was just so everyone else could hear me tell you that. Obviously, these murders are connected. I've been working the case and—"

"What?"

"Hanah's case. I've been working it on my own time and—"

"Stop."

"What?"

"Stop working that case. I had no idea you were doing this. Sweet Christmas, lady. It's going to end you up in a cell or dead or worse, same as me. Same as Humaid. That's why they did it. That's why they killed him. He kept going. He kept trying to find who really killed her. If they'll take out someone as rich and connected as him…they won't think twice about killing a cop."

"She was your wife, but she was my friend and I'm not going to just stand idly by and—"

"Afra!" I yell louder than is probably necessary.

"You're why I stopped."

She's taken aback by this. "What?"

"They got a message to me. Two months back or so. They said I had to stop digging or they wouldn't kill me. They'd kill you. So I did. I stopped. And I need you to stop, too."

She stares at me for a beat or two. And then she says, "No."

And the thing I hate most about everything in this moment is that she's right.

"Someone has to stand up to these people," she says with that ice in her veins I could never get enough of. "I'm not half the investigator you are, but if all I do is show up and try, then I'm twice the person."

And I know she won't stop. And I know she won't win. And I know I'll bury the only friend I have left.

Unless I win first.

There's gonna be a lot of blood in the sand.

Chapter 5

"All right," I say. "I'll do it. I'll find who killed them both. And, one way or another, I'll find justice for them. I'll hunt. But only if you drop this. Right now."

Afra doesn't for one moment doubt that I'm serious about starting back down the road that ruined my entire life. I've never lied to her, I'm not even sure I'd know how.

The problem is, I don't even know where to begin again. I stopped because they said they'd kill her. But the truth is, when I quit I was nowhere. I spent months running headfirst into brick walls only to find myself concussed and back at square one. Whoever did this is smarter than me and craftier than me. They're also richer than me and more connected but that's a bar so low a new-born sloth could clear it with ease. Any kid with a decent lemonade stand is richer and more connected than me.

"Okay," she says. "I'll back off. For now. As a favor to you because I think you could use someone who's on your side. But if you run into trouble you can't handle, I'm not afraid of these people."

"You should be," I say. "I am." And then I wonder what she means by that. "These people?" I say. "You have reason to think it's not one guy?"

She smiles. "I may have cracked that one thing. Maybe. Yeah. I don't think it's a serial killer like we thought. And even if I back off, there is one thing I can still do to help things along. There was this kid we picked up a couple of weeks back. He was Filipino. Still is, I guess. Anyway. Name is Manny. Short for Emmanual. We picked him up on about a hundred million counts of criminal computer fraud and abuse. Little turd hacked his way into everything from the video game servers to banks to food delivery apps so he could get free nachos."

"Nachos are good," I say thinking about how I haven't eaten in about a decade it seems. "And pretty overpriced."

She goes on. "While he was here, he said some stuff that I didn't really think was anything at first. Just rantings and ravings of a kid staring down the barrel of a long sentence before his life had really even begun. But the more I've thought about it…he can't be as crazy as he sounded and as scary with a keypad, I don't think. I know genius and madness go hand in hand, but not madness and writing a million lines of intricate code that the best tech guys in the world can't stop, right?" She pauses to consider just how insane she's about to sound. "He said something like," she adopts a terrible, nonsensical accent and says, "There's cults running around cutting out people's insides and you want to hassle me over chips and cheese. Sacré bleu!"

I can't help but laugh despite how awful everything is all the time. "Wait," I say. "Was that impression supposed to be the guy from Monty Python?"

"Yeah," she agrees excited that I noticed. "The one who farts in the general direction of the knights of the round table."

"That guy wasn't Filipino, Afra. He was French."

"I'm pretty sure you're wrong about that."

"He literally says, 'I'm French' at one point."

"Agree to disagree."

I laugh for a solid 30 seconds as she tries to thinks back the film. Then I try to remember the last time I laughed. Probably the last time I was with Afra.

"Look," she says, "are you telling this story or am I?"

I raise my palms to her as an apology and she soldiers on. "The point is, he was talking about cutting peoples' insides out. And that's…I mean that's pretty specific. We haven't seen much of that. Just the gallbladder and liver thing. A handful of murders including…you know."

I do in fact know. Someone cutting out the organs of your loved ones is not a detail one tends to forget.

"Once I put two and two together, I meant to interrogate him more about what he was talking about," she says, "but somehow all the evidence we had on him disappeared from our servers *while he was in custody*, the little weasel. So we had to let him go. Well, I say 'little.'"

"He had a partner? Someone on the outside who deleted the evidence"

"I think he had a computer on him that we didn't find when we searched him and booked him."

"How is that possible?"

"They make 'em crazy-small these days is all I'm saying."

And it takes me a minute to realize where she's going
with this. "You mean…up his…?"

"Best guess, partner. Anyway, I don't have anything to arrest him on, now. So he won't say a word to me. But I still know where to find him. You go have a conversation with him and it might just lead somewhere you've never been in this investigation."

"Okay," I say with more than a few hints of scepticism in my voice. "You sure he'll talk with me? I guess I could rough him up."

I don't like hurting people. But I'm pretty good at it. I've been big and hard my whole life and it's come in handy plenty, I must admit.

"I don't think you can," she says. And she slides her phone across the table open to a photograph.

And my eyes nearly bug out of my skull. She's right to use the word "kid." He can't be more than seventeen. And he looks like a sumo wrestler who at all the other sumo wrestlers. Except Filipino. He's 120 kilos if he's a gram.

"I didn't know they made orcas in the Philippines" I say. "So why is this guy gonna talk to me then?"

"Because he might want this back," she says. And she slides a tiny black sphere across the table to me.

It shines like it's wet even though it isn't, like a seal's skin. And it's maybe the size of a cough drop.

The look on my face must make it clear that I have no idea what she just handed me.

"This is some kind of…it's a skeleton key to the world is the best way I can describe it. This kid, Manny, he's some kind of next-level super genius apparently. And this thing is…it's an AI lockpick I think. Anything connected to a signal, WIFI or Bluetooth, radio, or whatever, it automatically connects to it and unlocks it. Doors, websites, email accounts, car engines, whatever. They make 'em crazy-small these days is all I'm saying."

"Well," I say, "this sounds like just about the most dangerous piece of tech I can imagine."

"Which is why it somehow accidentally didn't get logged into evidence after I recovered it at the scene. So there's no paper trail on it. It's clean to walk out of here."

"And you're just going to give this back to him? A criminal?"

"He made one, he can make more. Him having it back is less dangerous to me than a slimy lawyer or someone getting their hands on it in court. They get hold of it and suddenly all the evidence on ALL of their clients is gone somehow.

And now we've got muggers and murderers and worse back on the streets endlessly. A free pass to anyone who can afford it. Evidence walks away all the time. You know that. Might as well put it back where we got it."

That does make a weird kind of sense.

"Offer it back in exchange for all the information he has on the killings and maybe we'll get lucky. He can always make more, but surely he wants to know his competitors or enemies don't have one."

I pocket the sphere.

"And if you get caught with that, you have no idea where you got it, yeah?"

"Of course," I say.

"All right," she says standing. "I'm going to go get you released. We have literally nothing to hold you on. They just don't like you."

"Fair enough," I think as she heads out. "I don't much like me either."

She stops at the door, turns back, and says, "By the way. Happy birthday."

Chapter 6

I tracked Manny to the gaming cafe exactly where Afra said he'd be.

With his brain and his technology, Manny could be a millionaire or a billionaire. And heck, maybe he is. He could digitally walk into any bank or casino vault on the planet and no one could stop him. And he could make it like he was never there. And nobody would know. In his weird, teenage nerd way, Manny is by my estimation one of the most powerful people in the world right now.

But mostly he just likes to play video games and drink Mountain Dew, it seems.

I've been waiting for an audience with him for over an hour. He keeps telling me he'll be with me as soon as he's done "Pawning noobs."

If he actually talks like that or is just messing with me because I'm old and uncool I can't say. And I don't care.

Since I've been here he has eaten four pizzas.

I told him I have his incredibly dangerous tech and that I would return it to his giant person if he'd just stop farting around long enough to have a conversation. He just burped and said, "Yeah, bro. I'll be with you." He's even bigger in person. Too big the way a Clydesdale horse is too big. Like you just stare at him without wrapping your head around what you're seeing. The human brain just isn't wired to take in something like that. He's nearly impossible to process. He's not so much human as he is a gosh darn kaiju. He looks like a thousand bowling balls shoved in a tent made of tattooed skin. He looks like a major weather event. A tornado or a typhoon.

But what boggles the mind more than anything else is, he looks…like a kid. And he looks kind.

Still, part of me wants to fight him the way part of me would like to go back in time and fight Bruce Lee. Not because I think I could win, just for the story. But I don't have time to go to the hospital for several months right now.

I need him to be on my side, I need him to not shut down on me, but I also need to move my day along one whole heck of a lot faster than this.

"All right, Manny," I say. "I have an enormous gun and I'm about eleven seconds from shooting either you or your computer or both. I've had a crap day. I was chased by a naked man with a sword, my brother is dead, I was arrested for the one-millionth time for no reason, something pretty important keeps falling off my car, I missed my birthday dinner with my parents, and If I line it up just right I can take out my frustration on both you and your laptop with a single bullet."

He slowly turns his head and all seventeen chins to me and says, "Char?"

He's asking if I'm joking. I don't speak tagalong, but I picked up enough slang over the years to understand a fair amount of what the Filipino kids are saying. I don't say a word, I just pull back my coat and show off my Colt Python chambered in .357 magnum with a six-inch barrel, walnut stock, and cobalt blue steel. It fires 158-grain lead semi-wadcutter rounds more than 1,260 feet per second. And perhaps just as importantly, it's really scary looking.

It's not my usual carry, I made a special trip to my storage unit and dug this good boy out just for him. I've always heard it could stop a charging rhino and darn if I might just be about to find out.

His eyes go wide at the sight of the enormous hand cannon. But not in fear. In excitement. It's a weapon he's seen in movies and games come to life. "Petmalu!" he says. "That thing could maybe yeah get through even my hide!"

"Or, I say, I could just buy you lunch."

He smiles, "Get that credit card ready, brother. I'm not a cheap date." And he slaps his enormous belly. It sounds like thunder. It's louder than the booming laughter coming from his killer whale lungs. And I can't help myself. I kinda like this guy.

He wrestles his way out of a gaming chair that will never be the same after today and walks out the door.

Watching him go is maybe the strangest thing I've seen on a day made entirely of craziness. He moves like a panther.

I have to pick up the pace to catch up to him. How the devil does a man of his size move like that? If he told me he was secretly the world's best cat burglar I think I'd believe him. Nothing else makes sense so why should he, I guess.

When I catch up to him he can see the wonder on my face and he likes it. "Don't worry, brother, I'm not gonna really take you for all you're worth with this meal. 'Cause no offense, but I can see you ain't worth much."

"You're…not…wrong."

"I looked you up while I was playing. I'm a good multitasker. You used to be a cop and since then you've had more trouble with them than me. I like that about you."

"I like that about me, too," I say. "So…smart as you are, I don't suppose it takes much more than a google or two for you to know why I want to talk to you."

He shakes his head. "Not here." I nod.

We walk in silence for another three blocks until we come to a restaurant that could charitably be described as a "hole in the wall." There's no sign announcing what this place is. I doubt it even has a proper address. The kind of food you have to know about to know about. He has to turn sideways and squeeze to get through what passes for a door.

Once inside the seven people working or dining here all light up like roman candles. "Manny!" they yell like he's Norm coming into Cheers on the old American sitcom.

He waves one of his massive paws at them all as daintily as you like, like a princess in a parade saying hello to her passing subjects. And once again I don't know if it's a joke or if he's just this weird.

He removes a Zippo lighter from one of the fifty pockets on his vest and opens it, but doesn't strike it.

"Now there are no signals in or out of here. I've started disguising my tech as everyday items so people will hopefully stop taking it. Plus it makes me feel like James Bond."

I nod.

An elderly woman waddles out of the kitchen with two waters in her hands and a sour look etched between the cracks and fissures in her ancient face. "Manny! We need the internet for credit cards I keep telling you!"

Manny digs a roll of bills the size of a small dog out of his pocket and hands it to her. "Everybody is on me today." She smiles and nods. "You're a good boy, Emmanuel."

"You want your usual?"

"Yes, please, madam Lixue."

She nods and hurries away with more spring in her step than when she approached.

"What's your usual?" I ask.

"Everything!" He says with a rosy-cheeked, Santa Clause smile.

I genuinely can't help myself. I like this guy. "So," he says, contorting his jolly, Brobdingnagian features into something resembling a serious face. "You've heard about my hobby somehow. You heard I've been doing research and that know things about the killings and you want to know who killed your wife." "And her brother," I say. "My brother. He just died last night."

He nods solemnly. "Sorry for your loss. Here's the thing, though. I don't know nuthin' 'bout this cult, brother. Just rumors and hearsay and the like on the dark web. I've been trying but I've got almost zero concrete anythings." He leans in and whispers, "And if the rumors I hear are even half true, then even with my Zippo open, we shouldn't be talking 'bout them. 'Cause they got eyes and ears everywhere, bro. I honestly ain't even sure you're not one o' them."

"One of who?" I ask. "I investigated my wife's killing for months and I got nowhere, too. Partially, I think, because I was looking for a single killer. Now you're telling me it's a cult? Like…like devil worshipers or people trying to take a ride on a comet or something?"

"I don't know who or what they worship, bro. But I know they do got some ties to the stars. Or somethin'."

He dips his finger into his water and starts fiddling with the paper placemat in front of him. The one that every single Chinese restaurant in the world seems to use that shows the twelve signs of the Chinese zodiac starting with the rat and ending with the pig.

I'm a monkey but I always wanted to be a dragon.

"Give me a name. Please."

"I've said more than I should."

The ancient Chinese lady returns with forty-one takeout containers and places them on the table.

"I don't eat in front of people," he says. "I get self-conscious." He then takes his placemat and puts it in front of me. "You can finish my puzzle for me, yeah?" He stands up, grabs his boxes, and starts to leave. "Wait," I say. I take the small black orb Afra gave me from a pocket. "This is yours."

"Keep it, bro. Where you're going, it may be the only friend you'll have." And he's gone.

I hoped for answers. Now I've got even more questions. Some of them are good questions. Some of them seem real dumb. Like what puzzles can I finish?

This isn't the kind of placemat like at a Pizza Hut that has mazes and crosswords on it and stuff.

And then I see the watermarks he made on the paper. He drew an X over eleven of the zodiac signs.

He circled the snake.

Chapter 7

Before following up on Manny's puzzle, I decided it was only right that I stop by and see Humaid and Hanah's parents. Well, their adoptive parents.

Their birth parents were both killed in a plane crash when the kids were toddlers. That poor family. They were born with silver spoons in their mouths and cursed monkey paws in their hands, I swear.

At least they're all together now.

The couple that adopted them after the crash were family friends. Old money compared to most of the world, compared to Hana's people they may as well have just won the pick-six lotto last week. They didn't much care for me while Hanah was alive and they hated me with the fury of a thousand midday desert suns after she died. Truth be told, they're not good people. They knew I couldn't possibly have been responsible for Hanah's death and they led the charge to see me hanged anyway just because their pain needed somewhere to go, I guess. Better to let it burn me alive than hurt them.

That was the way my troubles with them ended. But they started long ago. We were locking horns from the moment I stole my first kiss from Hanah. They thought we weren't right for each other and our marriage could only be a disaster. Back when I bothered to hate things, I hated them for how hard they made it for us.

And I hated them even more for being right in the end.

They are terrible people.

But only a year after they lost their daughter they lost their son, and I should pay my respects. Even monsters deserve compassion.

I walk up the twenty-three steps leading toward the front door counting each one as I go. It's not an accident that this is a prime number. It's just an old man with enough money to design his house and his thoughts to pretend meaning exists where it does not.

When I reach the top I take four deep breaths. I haven't been here since my wife died. I would have paid my respects then, of course, but I was a little busy being railroaded for her murder.

I raise my fist, but I never actually knock.

Because before I can the door swings open with authority. And the very next thing I know two great apes in really expensive suits are carrying me back down the twenty-three steps. They smell like jasmine and heather honey.

When we're six steps from the ground they toss me the rest of the way. Something cracks when I hit the ground and I'm reminded I'm not nearly as young as I was when they used to toss me out of here once or twice a week.

"Wait!" I yell up at the fragrant gorillas as I still sit on the dusty ground.

They stop and turn their heads about a quarter of the way back toward me. Like they're listening but they can't be bothered to really pay attention.

"His place will be in Heaven," I say. "May Allah be merciful with him."

They both nod and head back up and into the house.

I dust off my pants and I dust off my cool. And before I head out I notice something at the bottom of the stairs. Something that wasn't there last time I came around. Two statues of roaring lions rampant on either side of the steps.

Carved from black marble. The same rock used to kill my wife.

Chapter 8

Black marble isn't unique. It isn't even rare. The entirety of the Taj Mahal is made of marble. As are many if not most kitchen countertops. Even a fair amount of iPhone cases these days are marble for people who want the ultimate luxury of their phone weighing six pounds.

Google tells me it's also hypoallergenic, so that's nice.

Whoever bashed my wife's head in with a rock was in little to no danger of sneezing.

Coincidences do happen. More than detective types would probably like to admit. Finding black marble in

Hanah's wounds and at her parents' house isn't a smoking gun. Correlation isn't the same as causation. And one of the harder things about being a detective is, when you deal with enough monsters you start seeing them under everybody's bed.

Marble in the wound and marble in their statue is

proof of nothing. But it's still a little weird. It's still something I'll have to look into further. At some point, I should decide if I want it to be them or not. It would be satisfying, in a way, but also extra sad I think.

I tell my phone to make a note about the statues but my phone still hates me and refuses to do it. It's probably just paranoia and exhaustion, but I swear I heard the thing laughing at me when I asked. So I make a note on a napkin as I wolf down a kebab and try to plan my next move.

Right now the priority is following up on Manny's lead, such as it is. A single placemat. So I head home. Well, I head to my parents' home. I had to move back in with them when everything in my entire life went sideways a year ago. Just one more thing that would make me irresistible to the ladies if I had any interest in not being resisted these days.

Something else falls off the car on the way back. Not sure what it was but it must have been pretty big judging by the way the guy behind me swerved and honked.

Amazing how much we can lose and still move forward. Always forward.

The house is small but cosy. When he was about my age, my father invested almost every penny of his considerable inheritance in making a kung fu movie that he also starred in. It didn't work out for a lot of reasons, not the least of which is because the man has never taken a single martial arts class or ever once been in a fight. He lost nearly everything. An outcome any child could see coming. And I'm not sure he ever cared.

My mom took what little was left and built a really nice life for us. And the first thing you see when you walk through the front door of their home is a six-foot poster of that movie. My dad, shirtless, photoshopped abs rippling on top of a pile of dead bad guys forty men deep. A very hot lady who is not my mom, her white dress strategically ripped in a few places, clings to his leg for dear life. And the title "Fury Fingers" in huge letters. The font isn't quite Comic Sans, but it's not far off enough, either.

The film currently holds a two percent rating on the review aggregator site Rotten Tomatoes because eighteen months ago a fourteen-year-old certified reviewer from Iowa gave it its first positive review in history. Dad threw a party that lasted a week and a half to celebrate.

I smile every time I come through the door.

The first thing you see in my parents' house is a monument to the most colossal failure of my father's life. And I respect the heck out of that. He tried to do the impossible and it didn't work out. It nearly ruined him. And he didn't run away from it. He framed it and gave it pride of place in his home.

That, in my estimation, makes him mighty.

They've both heard about Humaid's death and they give me hugs and offer me tea and ask me if I need anything. I thank them and tell them right now I just need rest. Which is the truth.

But I'm not going to get it. There's too much to be done and I may have my first solid lead yet in the only case that will ever really matter to me.

I lock myself in my childhood bedroom and start digging around the web as best I can. It seems unlikely that a murder cult has a website with a phone number and an address or something, but it's the 21st century and it's just about as unlikely that they have managed to go completely unnoticed in a world where virtually every one of the eight billion people on the planet is recording everything all the time.

Running internet searches for things like "snake cult" + "gallbladder" + "liver" will get you some weird results, man. First thing you gotta do with any off-the-wall search is filter out the porn.

Next, try to identify the whack job conspiracy theorists. The people who are also posting about lizard people running the world governments and how birds aren't real. Do just those two things and you'll find you've cut out about ninety-eight percent of the stuff on the web.

What remains may or may not be useful. Some of it is music that's not all that bad if you're into weird Swedish black metal.

An hour or so into scouring the web and I don't have any huge breaks or aha moments. But what almost immediately becomes clear is that this thing, whatever it is, is not limited to Dubai. It's not even local to The UAE, the Middle East, or Asia. Bodies have been dropping all over the world. Hundreds of them in what looks like basically every country on the planet.

Men and women. Wealthy and poor. Blondes brunettes and redheads. Short and tall. Skinny and heavy. Every race, creed, and color. Every kind of person you can think of is represented among the deceased. The only thing connecting them at all is that they were all missing two organs. And they all died within the last 11 months.

No one or two or ten people could pull this off. Maybe it's a cult. Maybe it's a paramilitary organization. I have no idea. But it's big and it's scary and I have no business taking them on.

But I'm sure going to anyway.

The first killing that fits the pattern was just after midnight on February ten.

Actually, the first twenty-one deaths were on February ten. Different times of day across eighteen countries.

Why? What triggered it?

Another quick Google tells me what was significant about that date: it was Chinese New Year.

As I turn all that around in my exhausted, addled brain I catch something out of the corner of my eye. The green light next to the camera on my laptop flashed for just a moment.

Someone is watching me.

Chapter 9

One of my searches tripped an alarm somewhere and now somebody is watching me. Anybody with an ounce of sense would probably close their laptop, chuck off the nearest skyscraper, and run until their shoes fall off.

I've been accused of a lot of things in my time, but having an over-abundance of sense is not one of them.

I'm no hacker, but any detective worth half a hill of beans in the 21st century has a suite of digital tools at the ready. I fire up a black market program called "Snooper Scooper" to find who accessed my camera. It should follow and back-trace anyone who is or has recently accessed my machine.

Immediately a screen pops up showing me a circular progress bar tracking how far along I am toward seeing who's spying on me. At this rate, I should know in about fifteen seconds.

And then a new screen appears. One I had nothing to do with. This one features a series of five metal doors, like something you'd see on a solitary confinement cell in a maximum-security prison. Each one says, in big block letters, FIREWALL.

Well, whoever is watching me has a flair for the dramatic. And they have me beat. Because clicking on this program was basically my only move here. I'm not a hacker. No way I'm getting through these firewalls. I'm honestly not even a hundred percent sure what a firewall is.

I give up. Again. I'm getting really good at it.

And then my leg feels weirdly warm.

And an icon pops up on my screen that says, "New device connected: Manny's A-bomb."

I pull the little orb from my pocket and it's not black anymore, it's kind of an electric blue. It feels like it's spinning even though it's not. And it's hot.

And one by one, the little doors on my screen fly open.

And little by little, my smile grows.

Whoever is on the other end must be pooping bricks.

And suddenly I have access to…everything. Everything on their computer. Emails, pictures of their kids, their dang Spotify playlists.

One guy keeps showing up in photos that zip across my screen. He looks like a tiny Arabic Wolverine from the X-Men movies.

Then the person watching me starts deleting things in a hurry.

I start downloading everything I can as the person on the other end starts wiping their hard drive as fast as they can. It's a race and I don't know everything I'm getting, but I know for sure I have their IP address, which tells me their geolocation. These jerks are less than forty blocks from me.

And then a box pops up asking me if I want to access their camera. Oh heck yes I do. I click the box and I'm staring at the man staring at me. He's wearing a mask. Either he just always wears that while spying on people or he knew there was a chance he'd be found out and planned ahead.

Hard to be sure over a webcam, but the mask seems to be made of human flesh.

We stare at one another for moments that feel like weeks. We're playing chicken, I think. That's a game I never lose. Because the key to winning a game of chicken is not caring if you live or die.

Without breaking my gaze, without so much as blinking, I reach across my desk and grab a sharpie and an old parking ticket. I scrawl a message in big, angry letters. And I hold it up to the camera.

It says, "I'm coming for you." He blinks.

Chapter 10

I don't know what I expected. An abandoned warehouse, maybe. Maybe a castle with a six-story snakehead carved at the top. What I found at the location the IP address sent me to was a luxury hotel.

Welcome to Dubai. Even the death cults are crazy rich and like a pool with a swim-up wet bar.

This is not great, though, because it could have been someone in any room on any floor of this enormous building that was spying on me. I take a quick look around the lobby, but sadly I don't see any big signs saying things like "Murder Cult: Room 207." It's not a needle in a haystack. It's a needle in a needlestack. If I had the manpower of the entire police force and if the person I'm hunting is very dumb then maybe, maybe, maybe, I'd find some evidence long after they'd fled the building. But I don't have that. I've got a smoker's cough, sleep deprivation, and a can-do spirit. Which all amounts to roughly nothing.

I'm just about to give up and spend my day looking through the files I grabbed off their server instead when someone gets off the elevator. He's short, stocky, and as hairy as anything. Like an Arab Wolverine. He looks around the room like he's checking for snipers. He clocks me almost immediately, bugs his eyes, takes off like a shot to the stairwell.

That's weird, right?

Why not just take the elevator all the way to wherever you're going in the first place?

Maybe the guy I'm hunting is pretty dumb after all.

Seems like a person worth following. So I follow.

In the stairwell, I can just make out his figure a couple of floors below me. He takes a door on basement level 3.

The doorknob is solid gold and ornamented. It looks like a simple circle embossed on the handle that doesn't quite close. But I look a little closer and there's a tiny serpent's head on one end of the loop. What are the chances that's a coincidence?

I get a firm grip on my Colt Python and, a little slower and warier than the guy I'm chasing, I take the same door. It's an amazingly heavy metal thing. Not unlike the ones that popped up on my screen a little bit ago.

Weirdly the whole floor is a single, huge room. Wires and papers and things are strewn haphazardly about the place. Like a lot of people just picked up every single everything and ran.

It still smells like people in here. Perfume, deodorant, sweat, and fast food. They left in the last half-hour, I'd guess. They left because I spooked them.

I can't help but smile at that.

And I can't help but think there may be footage of the ocean of scared people running away carrying computers and desks and phones. Probably they've got the sway to scrub the hotel security cameras. But tourists are shooting their vacations and teens are tiktoking their latest dance memes and taxis picking up and dropping off have their dash cams going. No way they could scrub them all. Not this fast and maybe not ever. I forced a huge error today.

As soon as I find those videos I can nail at least some of these crazies to the dang wall.

Today is a really good day.

But wait…if it's just a big open room…where did Wolverine go?

And then the door I came in shuts and locks.

All I can do is grit my teeth and accept just how dumb I am. It's a trap. Of course it is.

I try putting my shoulder to the door but it's made of iron or steel or something and it's much harder than me.

I look at my phone and this place is a dead zone. Of course it is. Or maybe my phone just hates me so much it finally found an opportunity to get rid of me for good.

Well…crap. Today is a bad day.

And then a secret panel opens in the wall. Because what's a creepy murder cult without secret panels in walls?

Five men in long red robes walk from the secret hole about ten meters from me. Their faces are covered in solid gold snake masks, blood-red rubies for eyes.

They're all carrying huge silver scimitars and I can tell from here how sharp they are. The swords seem to cut the air as they move slowly toward me each step precisely in unison.

There are five of them? That's fine. I've got six bullets.

"Guys," I say, raising my still-enormous pistol. "Don't know if you ever saw Indiana Jones but the guy with the gun wins."

They don't say a word. They don't slow down. They just march toward me in lockstep.

"I need some answers," I say, pulling the hammer back on my hand cannon. "I don't need bodies. You guys don't have to die today."

They keep marching. Each step from each man landing at once. Silent as the grave. Swords gleaming. "Come on, guys. Lay down your weapons. Last chance."

One more march toward me. They're too close and I don't have any more room to retreat. I'm out of options.

I fire on the serpent on the far left. He flies back like he was hit by a truck. The other four still march forward. What the hell is this?

I fire again. Again a man falls dead.

Again they march.

Again.

Again.

Again.

I shoot dead all five men. And I scream to the ceiling because I assume someone is watching, "What was the point of that? Did you just hate these guys? Let me go!"

And the panel opens again.

And five more snakes in red robes step out.

And now I have one bullet left.

And all at once, they march toward me.

My first thought is if they kill me they can't get Manny's A-bomb. So I do the only thing I can think of, I swallow it.

It hurts going down, but I have a feeling that's just the beginning of the hurt I'm in for.

I run through my choices.

I shoot one and then pick up a sword and try to cut the other four down like I'm Darth bloody Vader. Not sure I've ever held a sword in my life and even if I win. What then? Another five snakes walk out of the wall?

I know I'm not getting through that metal door. What's on the other side of the opposite wall? The underground parking garage, right? This is going to hurt.

This is a very bad day.

I sprint with all the speed I can muster and I leap into the wall.

It gives.

The sheetrock shatters, I tear through some wires, and the fiberglass insulation wraps around me, blinding me and cutting me as I sail through.

I slam into a concrete wall on the other side and I fall.

And fall.

I fall two stories until I land on a Vinci Model Q shattering the windshield and three of my ribs.

No time to bleed.

No time to look for my awful car.

I throw off the pink insulation and climb into the insanely fancy electric car using the hole my body made in the windshield. I frantically dig through the glove box and center console and the sun visors looking for a valet key but I don't find one.

I can't outrun these guys on foot. Not with broken bones.

And then I have to fight like crazy to stop myself from puking. My stomach feels like it's spinning. It's hot. I may vomit in the most expensive car in the world. I grip the dash to steady myself. It's the darkest, smoothest wood I've ever felt. And there's a word carved into it but my head is spinning too hard to read. "Quesedilla" or something. That can't be right.

This isn't working I have to—

And the car's ignition turns over.

Manny's A-bomb started the car from inside me. I knew I liked that guy.

I throw the car into reverse and fly out of the parking spot.

As soon as I do I'm t-boned by a Range Rover.

My head hits the window hard enough to break the glass and definitely fracture my skull.

No time for concussions.

I shift into drive and punch it.

I wipe the blood out of my eyes.

More blood just takes its place.

It runs down my face and neck and pools onto the black leather seat which, frankly, is super comfortable.

The Rover gives chase.

At the entrance, there's a line of cars coming into the lot and a line going out. But the little machine that you pay, that thing's just made of aluminium. I thread the needle between the two lines of cars and tear through the ticket machine like I'm opening a baked potato.

And I burst out onto the street.

And two more black SUVs join the Range Rover that tried to kill me a few seconds back.

Even with the damage I'm carrying, I'm faster than them, but I'm not faster than their network. They can call who knows how many more cars to follow and to pursue from every direction and to eventually box me in. I need to get off the road fast.

Where are you going, detective?

I guess it's time to bring Afra back in on this and hope she can do things I can't before any corrupt higher-ups shut her down. I've got the files I grabbed from them on a jump drive in my pocket. And I'm only ten or so blocks from her office. Even if these snakes kill me, at least I'll hand this off to her, start what will hopefully be the end of this cult, and maybe even say goodbye to the only friend I've got. The girl who, if we're being honest in what could be the last few moments of my life, probably should have been THE girl.

I loved Hanah and I'll always love Hanah. Not sure she could say the same about me but that's for her to decide. But the moment I met Afra I was pretty sure I had no idea what love could have been like. The first time I made Afra laugh I was pretty sure it was the only sound I ever wanted to hear again.

I make a promise to myself to see if she and I could be something else if I make it out of this. And then…I don't make it out of this.

The SUVs fall back a little.

Traffic seems to stop ahead.

A garbage truck comes from my left side. I don't have time to react. I only see it for a nanosecond.

And then I don't see anything at all.

Chapter 11

It's dark. Blacker than black. Vantablack. There is no definition to anything. No differentiation. Just flat, endless dark.

Where am I? What is this?

And it's cold. Holy balls is it cold. Colder than anybody who grew up in a desert can even begin to imagine. So cold I can't focus. Can't think. Can't move.

I feel like I could break at any moment. Like an old leather shoe dipped in liquid nitrogen. Drop me and I'd shatter.

Am I in a box?

Am I in a coffin?

Am I dead?

What do you remember? The thing coming from the left. What thing? What left?

Who even are you?

You're a detective, right? An Emirati. A...A truck!

I was hit by a truck.

Dead makes a lot of sense after that memory.

Is that a memory or a story? Are those two things even different in any appreciable way?

Why would being dead feel this cold?

Because you don't have whatever organs working you need to keep you at nighty-eight point six? It's circulation, right. The heart pumping. That's what keeps you warm. Dead bodies cool at one to two degrees an hour. To be this cold I'd have to be dead for about a thousand years.

No. You'd just be room temperature, right?

No. You'd decay, dummy.

Unless someone put you in a freezer.

I was working on something. A case. Something about livers and gallbladders maybe. I can't see and I can't move but I can hear something. A hissing sound. Not like a snake but like the pneumatic compressed air brakes on a big truck. Like something *releasing*.

I went snowboarding once. At the mall. There's a whole ski resort in the mall right next to the food court and the Footlocker or whatever. 22,500 square meters of indoor skiing with a lodge and a lift and fresh powder year-round. The whole deal. They keep the place at negative one degree Celsius. I ate it coming down the bunny slope. Hit the ground headfirst at speed and got snow in my pants, in my underwear, in all the nooks and crannies where you don't want frozen water. It was the only time I remember really understanding how much cold can hurt.

It was a hot tub compared to this.

Why did you remember that? Focus. I can't focus. Too cold to focus.

I was with a writer once. A great one. It was below freezing. He had a cup of boiling water and we went outside and he threw it into the air and the boiling water immediately became snow.

It's colder than that.

Wait. No. I wasn't there. I've never been wherever it gets that cold, have I?

There were gunshots in the woods that night. The thing…the…cult? There's a cult somewhere. Am I in a cult?

Not gunshots. Trees exploding. We were under attack? Mortar? No. The branches were breaking from the inside. The sap was expanding and blowing out the branches from within. That's how cold it was.

He wrote about death and honey and stardust.

I've never been where it was that cold.

I saw it on YouTube. Right?

This is colder.

Did I even ever snowboard, then? Am I a detective?

Every problem has a solution. There's a way out of this box. Even if I am dead. Even if I'm not sure what memories are real. Even if I'm not 100% sure who I am. Even if it's the dang great beyond on the other side of this door, everything begins with getting out of the coffin.

Not a coffin. A freezer. Right? Has to be. Right?

Why would they put me in a freezer if I were dead? To stop me from smelling.

Why would I be wondering why I'm in a freezer if I were dead? I don't know. I've never been dead before.

I broke my ribs. I remember now. Falling. I fell on a…something. A car. Three ribs broke.

It's not easy but even in a space this cramped, and even this cold, I can just manage to manoeuvre my hand enough to feel my side. Fingers are numb. Everything is numb. Hard to say for but sure nothing hurts. I mean, everything hurts because I'm frozen. But my ribs are fine I think.

Maybe that was just a movie, too. Maybe I'm a banker or a chef or maybe I was never alive at all. Maybe none of us ever were. I'm thinking. Am, therefore, I?

I smell the air and it smells like nothing. Like too much nothing. Like someone put the nothing there on purpose if that makes sense. Which it doesn't.

I move one hand to the opposite wrist and check my pulse. It's there. Barely. Maybe twenty beats a minute. Maybe ten. Too cold to keep a solid count. Too cold to focus. But I must be alive.

I hear something. Something crackling like logs in a fire. Like the tree branches just before they exploded. I try to follow the sound as it echoes around the box. Try to follow it back home.

It's my lungs. My lungs are breaking tiny sheets of ice inside my chest as they expand and contract. I'm breathing. I must be alive.

I try to taste the air. It just tastes like cold. Like fresh, undriven cold.

I use my tongue to count my teeth. There's twenty-eight of them. Twenty-eight? What the hell is happening?

That's one too many teeth.

That memory is real. I'm sure of it. I don't know why I'm sure of it. But it has to be.

I lost a tooth running down a meathead who put his own mom in hospital six years ago. She was in her sixties. Had died red hair. He broke her nose and her eye socket for her pitiful pay check. She earned something like fifty dollars a day selling fish at a market and he wanted that fifty dollars enough to hospitalize his own mom.

I tracked him to one of the usual spots people go when they're the kind of people who hit their moms for drug money. He ran. He was pretty fast for a junkie. But I was faster. And he was dumb, of course. Went down a blind alley with no exit. Had to get through me if ever wanted to be free to hurt little old ladies again.

There was no way he was getting through me.

He was high as a paper kite, feeling no pain, and got lucky with a right cross when I cornered him behind a Thai place downtown. Really good noodles at that place.

Memory is starting to come back. To feel real. To feel sure.

He wore a class ring. His fake ruby took a molar out of my upper jaw. But I put him down after that. I slipped his next shot, ducked a haymaker, and came up bringing with me maybe the best uppercut I've ever thrown. Really got my legs into that one.

I spat out that tooth and it got lost among the twelve or thirteen his sins cost him that day.

Yeah. I remember. That was a good fight.

Voices.

I'm hearing voices that I'm pretty sure aren't in my head. They sound a hundred miles away but that's probably just because I'm in some kind of freezer coffin. The sound can't travel through the steel or through the cold or both.

At absolute zero, even light can't move through. It just stands there still and frozen as an icicle on an arctic eave. Like a laser blast caught by a Jedi. I remember those movies. I remember they aren't real. I must have watched them a hundred times as a kid. Feet feeling under me now.

Why would they kill me, fix my tooth, and put me in a freezer?

I'm not yet prepared to say this is the weirdest day of my life but that's just because I'm pretty sure I once sang karaoke with Prince.

Or was it a prince impersonator?

Or did I just see a music video?

The fog seems to come and go. Can't cut it. Don't have the right knife. I don't have any knife. I don't have any tools.

Wait.

I don't have pants.

How did it take me this long to realize I'm naked?

How long has it been? How long does it take to think? Are memories slower in the cold, too? Like water. Like light.

I should scream for help. There's no shame in it even though it feels like there's *only* shame in it.

I try.

I can't.

Guess my voice is frozen, too. Words can't push through the ice.

And then there's a crash, like medieval swords clanging together.

The snake people had swords.

Snake people? What the hell am I remembering? And then there's light. Lines of lightning ripping the dark into pieces. Then there's a ball of light. Then there's only light. Like waking up on the surface of the dang sun.

I close my eyes and I turn away as best I can.

It burns. It's the only thing in my world that isn't frozen.

And then a voice I've never heard before says something. What is it? She speaks softly and calmly like she's trying to soothe a big cat.

"Can you hear me?" she asks. I feel like I'm a hundred meters below her in a well.

"Hello? Can you move? Can you hear me?"

I turn my head back and fight the light as hard as I've ever fought anything in my life. She's a blur, but a human-shaped blur I'm pretty sure. Long black hair. She's white. Too white. Ghostly white.

No. That's her clothes. It's a lab coat. She's a doctor or something.

"You're going to be okay," she says. "I know it's a lot, but you're alive and you're okay." She says to someone else, "Get the warming blankets and some tea. Sleepy Time, I'm told is preferred." She knows what kind of tea I like.

Wait. I know what kind of tea I like.

"My name is Mary," she says. "I'm here to help."

The room starts to come into focus a little. My lungs stop crackling. Pins and needles everywhere. Like every nerve in my body is waking all at once. Because they are.

"Where am I?" I manage to croak out dryly.

I can see Mary enough to see her smile. It's a pretty smile. A kind smile. A practiced smile.

"Khalifa bin Ahmed," she says. "Welcome to the year 2122."

Chapter 12

Mary talks. A lot.

I do my best to keep up but for long stretches I do what I do best, I give up. She never seems to notice or slow down. She's like a podcast you listen to at 2x speed. A human chainsaw of words.

She says something about cryogenics and she's very sorry to have to tell me but I really am still alive.

She speaks English not like an Emirati or anyone else I know. The people I grew up with, we mostly sound like we learned English from watching reruns of American TV from the 90s. Because we did. She speaks like she was born in a lab run by the Duolingo owl or something. It's flawless. No hint of an accent. Like she's the lady who does all those YouTube videos that teach you how to pronounce the words you've only ever read, never heard spoken aloud.

I want to ask her to say "synecdoche" but I don't.

She has feral eyes and long hair almost as black as the world I just came out of. She has skin like someone wove caramel into silk. She smiles like an ivory train track. I fight to convince myself she's not a dream.

I don't trust her to be real.

I don't trust her to be on my side. Whatever side that is.

She puts a thing that looks like a small hammer on my arm and says, "This will warm you up." Something makes a faint *tsss* SOUND AND almost immediately I stop shivering. I feel human-ish.

"And this," she says, "should help with the grogginess." Another *tsss* and I feel like I just had six cups of coffee and a vacation.

She reaches in to get me. I'm a frozen ragdoll. Can't move. Can't speak. I'm a sitting duck.

After maybe three minutes and two hundred thousand words, she gets me out of the box just a little and I'm in what can only be described as a mass grave, I think. I look around as best I can and I'm staring at death stacked on death. Only a half dozen or so boxes like mine were uncovered by the three or four-meter hole Mary dug to get me out, but there are hundreds more here lost to the sand and the century. Thousands, maybe. You can feel it.

I was buried in a potter's field, I guess.

"Take all the time you need to get your feet under you," she says, "but also we really need to hurry. If we're found out here…" She trails off and the fear in her voice is real enough that it chills me despite whatever elixir she just shot into my apparently ancient veins. "I have one more shot for you but you're not going to like it."

"Then let's don't," I say. Or I try to say. Not sure what came out.

"It's important," she says, placing the hammer-thing back on my arm. "You're not emetophobic, are you?"

"Give me a sec to look it up and I'll tell you."

"Go on ahead and lean over the side of the cryochamber."

I do as I'm asked because what the heck at this point. Another tss and I immediately start retching, convulsing, and vomiting again and again. I feel like I'm trying to throw up every single one of my organs all at once.

"What!" Vomit.

"The!" Vomit.

"Hell!" Vomit.

"Sorry, sorry, sorry!" She says and she looks like she means it behind those wildcat eyes. "I'll explain on the way."

She tries to pull me out of the box bodily, but I've got about a hundred pounds on her and it's like watching a new-born try to wrestle a bag of potatoes. From inside the bag.

"A little help here, Khalifa!"

I try to get my legs to listen to me and it doesn't go great. It's like a new-born giraffe trying to stand for the first time on a frozen lake.

"I'm sorry to rush you. I know this must be hard. You haven't actually used those muscles in a hundred years," she says as she tries to guide me toward a small ladder. "But I didn't save your life just to get us killed by them. So we really do have to move."

There's simply no way this person is telling me the truth about any of this. But I'm weak as a kitten and still too addled to run or fight or even complain much.

With a lot of help and cursing, I climb out of my grave.

When I'm topside, she loads me into a truck. It's not even remotely a flying truck so I know the whole 'this is the future' thing must be malarky. She tears off through the sands at what feels like about two hundred kilometres an hour. I check the speedometer on the dash and I'm wrong. We're doing 220. And the display is a hologram. And Mary isn't touching the wheel. So maybe I'm really not in the 2020s anymore. Or maybe it's all an elaborate trick.

Maybe I really am dead.

I'm too tired to care, I think.

There's a sand storm kicking up. At least the desert is still here. Some things are eternal, I guess.

"The storm is just starting," she says. "It'll provide a little cover for us to move about."

"So we've got three more days of cover for whatever we need cover for."

She smiles. "Yes. Storms are always three days. Just like a century ago. Nice that some things don't change."

"What was that place?" I ask. "Where am I?"

She explains everything as best she can. When the truck hit me it basically liquified my insides. "You never actually died like almost all the people in that graveyard, but it was close. You were in hospital for years, a vegetable with no hope of recovery. Your parents, they did everything that could be done but you lived in a primitive time, no offense."

I fought meth heads in alleyways for a living so no offense is taken.

She goes on, "They were going to pull the plug on you. Your funeral was even planned. I'm told it was going to be lovely. But then someone mentioned cryogenics."

"Freezing me," I say or maybe I ask. "Like a storebought lasagna."

"Keeping you in stasis at extremely low temperature until medical technology advanced enough that you could be brought back out safely. It was new, then. Newish. Still in its infancy. But they had the first part worked out well enough. They could essentially put you in suspended animation indefinitely"

"They just put me on ice and threw me down into time. A frozen coin in a wishing well," I say, still not buying all this. And then something occurs to me. "Wait. Not like a lasagna. Like a *very* expensive lasagna. I don't have that kind of cash. Neither do my parents. So…"

"An anonymous benefactor came to your aid."

"Who?"

"My dad, actually."

"Who is your—"

"You'll meet him. Again."

I don't much like mysteries. You might think that would make me a bad detective, but I think it actually is what made me slightly better than okay at my job. I hate not knowing stuff so much that I dig and I hound and I fight until I know it. I guess I'll figure this one out soon enough.

"So If I was frozen by an anonymous benefactor…why was I in a hole in the ground?"

"Cryonics became popular around the 2020s and stayed popular for a few decades I guess. Not long, really. We made enough advancements that people who could afford to freeze themselves for later could afford better longevity tech. And after a while, we advanced far enough that most people who were frozen could be brought back."

I start to get a sense of where this is going. "So at that point, everyone who had family with the pull and the power to bring their loved ones back did."

"You *are* a detective."

"But the people who were on their own, and the people who had family who thought they were better off without mom and dad or whatever…" "Yes," she says.

"We got left on a shelf. Why bother doing the work if nobody is making you."

"Bingo, my new popsicle friend. Thousands of men and women were just abandoned to time. There was outrage about it for a while but then there was something new to be outraged about. Eventually, the cryo chambers were taken out of storage and just buried in the sand. They ran off tiny fusion reactors which could keep you all in stasis virtually forever, so it's not like it was murder. And even if it was murder…almost all of you were already dead."

"I get it. The world still sucks."

"You have no idea. But you're about to."

"What I don't get is this: why do I have too many teeth?"

"Come again?"

"When I was in my accident last…uh…century, I was missing a tooth. Now I'm not."

"Oh! So before I cracked you open I flooded your chamber with nanobots programmed to fix anything that was wrong with you. That included growing you a new tooth. Fixing any scarring. Cleaning up any inflammation. And that's why I had to make you vomit like a freshman on prom night. Had to get the bots out of your system. They're miracle workers, but too long inside of you and they…do too much. Let's put it that way. Anyway. The good news is, you're gonna feel like you're eighteen again, my guy. I always do." "You are about eighteen, aren't you?" I ask looking her up and down a little more than is probably halal. I could be off by a few years. If she eats right and exercises like crazy and moisturizes like there's no tomorrow, maybe she could be twenty-three twenty-four.

Mary smiles that electric white smile. "I'm sixty-seven." I guess my eyes go a little wide 'cause she laughs at me and smirks. "Don't look at me like that, old man. You're 130, remember?"

And that doesn't really have time to sink in because of the blue lights behind us. Cops.

I turn to look and the police car really is flying. "Well," Mary says, "You may have been better off dead."

Chapter 13

There are a few things you want to see in a good car chase scene. You want some incredibly skilled driving, right? Down-shifting, and working the clutch like a concert pianist as you pull the E-brake and jerk the wheel to drift around tight corners and pull a one-eighty or two while weaving through traffic and pedestrians and cafe tables. Maybe you smash through a fruit stand, down a few hundred stairs, off a bridge, and onto the top of a passing truck.

Nonstop, pulse-pounding, edge-of-your-seat action where one wrong turn, one single moment of distraction could cost the hero her life or imperil the critical, world-saving mission.

Landmarks are great for a car chase because they look cool and give you a sense of where you are and how much distance there is between the predator and the prey. So throw as many of those bad boys in there as you can get away with.

Zip past the Leaning Tower of Pisa, leap over the Great Wall of China, fly through the Arc de Triomphe doing ninety while trailing a bank vault with Interpol hot on your heels.

Beyond the action, though, you want clean motivations for the chase and clear stakes. Why are we on the run? Who is trying to catch us? What happens if our heroes get caught or our bad guys get away?

My current chase scene is taking place in the middle of the desert. We're just running as fast as we can through emptiness and away from some flying thing.

There's no one and nothing around for maybe a hundred miles but sand. No traffic, no landmarks, no corners or stairs or anything.

I'm participating in the dang thing and I have no idea what the stakes or the motivation are. So all in all I'd say this one is not going great so far.

"There's nowhere to hide!" Mary says after she spends a while cursing in English, Spanish, and Chinese.

She hammers the accelerator and the machine giving chase easily matches our speed.

To make things even more fun, the sand storm is starting to roll in like it means it, now. It's coming on an east wind, at least forty kilometres an hour. I can't see the edges but I'd guess it's a few hundred kilometres wide. Maybe two kilometres tall. It's a big boy. We're moving west and we're going a lot faster than forty kph, so we should get to shelter before things get too dicey. As long as these idiots don't get us killed first. "Can we outrun them?" I ask, a little more alert and mobile enough to climb, with great effort, into the clothes Mary brought me, though still not aware enough to really know what it is I'm putting on.

She just looks at me like I'm an idiot. And I am, I never once denied that. But this one time it's also not entirely my fault I woke up a century after I went to sleep. Even Rip Van Winkle only did a twenty-year bid in dreamland. Maybe give me a full half-hour to get my bearings.

"Well," I say. "Then how do we take it down?" "No one has ever taken one down," she says. "They're hundred-million-dollar killing machines. They can't be stopped."

Well. Crap. "Why are the police even after us? Is it illegal to wake me up?"

A booming robotic voice hammers through the car, "Pull to the side of the road and turn off your engine."

"That's not the police. It's a corporate compliance drone. And yes it was illegal to wake you up. Crazy illegal. Honestly, you shouldn't have let me do it. I don't know what you were thinking. I'll explain more if we live long enough for it to matter."

"Pull to the side of the road or countermeasures will be deployed!"

"What happens if they catch us?" I ask.

"If we're very, very lucky, they'll kill us before they interrogate us."

I'm trying to take it all in and it's not working great. "Listen," she says, swerving on and off the road. "The future is worse and more dangerous than you can imagine. Trust nothing and no one. You hear me? No one."

The flying machine moves to our side and I get a pretty solid look at it. It's kind of shaped like a torpedo had a baby with a quadcopter. It has four rotors roughly where wheels would be if this were a Formula One car. "It's a drone," I say with a smile. "So no humans on board?" I start digging around under the seat.

"What are you looking for?"

"I imagine I'll know it when I see it." I pull out an emergency kit and quickly riffle through it. Road flares, tire gauge, fire extinguisher, compass, first aid kit, duct tape. I have to laugh when I see the little packet of kitty litter. That's there to help wheels get traction in the snow. Snow. A constant problem in Dubai.

At least she brought more sand to the desert. Then I do see it. A wheel wrench. It's heavy and it shines like salvation.

"Get me close to the drone!" I say.

"What? No. Away from the drone is what we're looking for here. So whatever your plan is, it's bad and we should do the opposite. What's the opposite?"

"I don't know. Die."

"That's my plan! We can't both have the same plan!" "This is your final warning," the robot voice commands. "You have sixty seconds to comply."

"Look," I say. "When I was on the force we had some surveillance drones. They were smaller than this thing, but the build was pretty similar. And you know what the biggest threat was? The thing that took them down more often than anything else?"

"You explaining things too long?" She says begging the car to go faster.

"Birds. It was what they call bird strike. A palm dove or a lapwing would kamikaze right into one of the rotors and that was all she wrote. A ten thousand dollar drone undone by a five-ounce bird that couldn't even carry a one pound coconut if it tried."

"Were you always this weird or is this a side effect of being dead for a century?"

"I'm going to shove a wrench in one of the thing's rotors. Wrench strike."

"Those rotors are titanium alloy. The hardest thing man ever created!" she whines.

"Do you have any plan other than complain and die?"

"Yes! No. Shut Up!"

"Then get me close!" I shout.

She hates it but she doesn't have a better idea. She slowly swings the truck closer and closer to the drone.

I open the sunroof and immediately the car starts to fill with angry desert sand. It whips at my face, feels like I'm a pot being scrubbed with steel wool.

When she's close enough I hurl the wrench into the front left turbine and it is immediately ejected, shot back into the car through the passenger window and out through the driver's window. It misses Mary's head by about a half-centimetre.

"Sweet forking Christmas, dude!" She shrieks as I climb back into the car. "Was your plan secretly to save time by killing me yourself?"

I cringe a bit. "Sorry! That was surprising."

"Not to me! I told you it wouldn't work."

"Well, it's nice to see nagging hasn't gone extinct in the 22nd century!" I start digging through the emergency kit again.

"Active measures begin in 20 seconds. To avoid likely death, pull the vehicle to the side of the road and turn off your engine."

"Duct tape!" I say. "There's never been a problem so big or complex it can't be solved with duct tape!" "I fundamentally disagree!" Mary says, panic all but consuming her.

I smile. "What's the matter, Mary? You want to live forever?"

She cocks her head and smiles that spotlight smile for the first time since the blue lights showed up. "Do whatever you gotta do, detective. I'll be over here praying."

I grab the tire gauge and pass it through the hole in the roll of duct tape. I pull about six feet of tape from the roll and wrap the first few centimeters of tape around a pair of scissors from the first aid kit for a little weight. I climb back out of the sunroof. The sand hammering my skin has not gotten any more pleasant.

As I recall, here's roughly how a helicopter works: In order for something to fly it has to achieve lift. And lift is made by wings. Birds do it, bees do it, even educated killer robots do it apparently.

Wings work by moving air along them faster on the bottom than the top. The faster air below creates a sort of suction on top of the wing creating lift and making it move upward.

The wings of a helicopter work exactly the same way the wings of a plane or a pigeon do, they're just spinning around rather than fixed on the sides.

This, believe it or not, was all more or less worked out by Leonardo da Vinci in 1489 when he invented the first helicopter. He called it the "Aerial Screw." That isn't important to the story but dang. You gotta respect the mind.

The important part of that story is that the rotors create suction from the top. If I can get my tape near one, physics should do the rest for me.

So I toss my duct tape strip toward one rotor and I hold my reel by the tire gauge like I'm trying to catch a marlin. I'm fishing for salvation. But, really, aren't we all?

It's nearly impossible to see in the dust, and we're moving crazy fast, and the wind is whipping this way and that. And Mary is yelling something but heck if I can hear a word of it.

Two pretty big guns appear from the front of the drone. I guess that's what they meant by 'active measures.' This is fine.

I pull and jerk and wrangle my line. I give it a little more slack. "Come on! Come on!"

"Firing in ten. Nine," the robot voice says.

I climb farther out of the sunroof. One good bump and I'm roadkill and I guess that's okay. I'm already dead.

"Eight. Seven."

I grit my teeth and shift my weight. The tape seems caught in the copter's vortex.

"Six. Five."

I give it a little more line and it catches! The front left rotor grabs the line and starts pulling.

"Four. Three."

It's ripping the tape so fast and so hard it's all I can do to hold onto the tire gauge. My forearms are burning. I think my hands are bleeding.

The tape is almost gone, the entire reel wrapped around that rotor.

"Two. One."

Well. I tried at least. Guess it didn't—

The rotor explodes! The heat and the force of the shock wave coming off it throws me back inside the car. I turn and watch the drone tumble and crash behind us.

Mary laughs a full-belly victory laugh and I can't help but join in a little.

"You just did the impossible, Iceman. Not too shabby. I knew I woke you up for a reason."

I look into those feral eyes and I may be dead but I'm not dead. I could get lost in them. I guess even in the far-flung future it always feels good to impress a pretty girl.

"Looks like we're gonna make it," she says. And that's when three more drones sweep in behind us.

Chapter 14

I woke up in the future and so far it's not great. We're boxed in on three sides by three drones that want two people dead for at least one reason I do not yet understand.

"Got any more magic tricks in that box of yours?" Mary asks.

I shake my head. I'm all out of duct tape and thinking we're about out of time. "I barely got one of these things last time. Taking out three seems…improbable."

Mary starts to cry just a little. Two little streams of tears carving a path down her flawless cheeks. "I'm sorry. I'm so sorry. I should have left well enough alone." She's quiet for a second. "My dad is gonna kill me so hard when he finds out I'm dead."

The robot voice is back telling us to comply, only now it's in surround sound. Three drones talking perfectly in sync with one another.

This time I notice the brand name stamped on one of them. Allied Scientific Progress. I don't know what that is, but I hate it.

I frantically look around the car, more eager to save this girl I've known for fifteen minutes than to save myself. Everything I love has been gone for a century. And even when I wasn't lost to time, I was well and truly lost. Nobody is going to miss me, including me.

But someone this beautiful shouldn't die. Maybe that's sexist or some other kind of bigoted. I don't know.

Nothing else in the car is sparking joy, though. I've got nothing to work with.

The robots tell us we have sixty seconds. I've heard it all before.

"Sorry I'm crying," Mary says. "I'm just not used to this stuff. Adventure really isn't in my nature. Being outside isn't even really in my nature."

And it's like a cartoon light bulb goes off above my head. "Nature," I say.

"Yeah? So?"

I tilt the rear-view mirror to look at the wall of sand chasing us and this terrible awful no good thought feels like as good an idea as any. We've been bobbing and weaving to try and shake the drone and it's slowed us down. The sand is hot on our heels. It could work.

"Turn into the storm," I say.

"Do what to the where now?" Mary says in disbelief. I guess they don't make my brand of crazy anymore.

"I don't know what kind of sensors these things are using to track us, but I bet even in the future they won't be able to work inside a sand storm."

"Neither will the car or our central nervous systems soon enough, bro!" She protests.

And the robots start counting down again.

Ten.

Nine.

"We'll make it longer than them. Trust me."

She looks at me and she's trying really hard to trust me. But it's just not happening. Eight.

Seven.

"It's sand or bullets, Mary!" I shout.

She screams in frustration and jerks the wheel hard to the left.

The peddle is already on the floor but she punches it again I guess for effect.

Six.

Five.

"I hope you know what you're doing," she says.

"Me too." Four.

Three.

The wall of wind and sand rushes at us and we rush right back at it.

Two.

One.

And we hit the storm. We disappear into it. We are swallowed by it.

The drones zoom in after us and are immediately lost to us. I can only hope we are also lost to them.

Visibility is zero here. The sound is bonkers. Deafening. Like we're tumbling inside a clothes dryer that's inside a double kick drum and the drummer is amped up on all of the cocaine.

The car immediately starts filling with sand so we close the vents. It helps but it doesn't stop it. The waterfalls of sand become trickles.

The displays in the car flicker and spasm. The computer that controls the car is getting absolutely brutalized, but the engine is still going for now. I feel our speed cut in half or more, but I think that's just

Mary being scared or smart or both. We don't need to be in the middle of this thing, we just need it to kick the beans out of some evil robots and get the heck out.

Mary has to shout at the top of her lungs to be heard. "The engine is starting to redline! We gotta get out of here!"

"Then do it!" If the murder copters aren't done and dusted by now we're toast either way.

"I'm turned around!" She shouts. "How do I know which way to go?" "Head west!"

"How the heck do I know what west is? The displays are down and I can't see the sky! I can barely see you!"

I dig through the sand dunes building on the floorboards and find the emergency kit. I brush it off and retrieve the compass. I point to my left and shout, "West!" Mary looks very confused. "We can't trust electronics out here!" "This is a compass."

"Like on my phone! I know but—"

I interrupt even though it's rude because time is of the essence here. "It's magnetic. Unless the north pole has been moved in the future it's fine!"

The threads tying her trust together are being stretched about as tight and thin as they can go without breaking, and I guess magnetic compasses aren't real prevalent in this new world, but she doesn't have much choice. She turns left.

"Now straighten it out." She does.

She's still afraid and going easy on the accelerator, though.

"It's going to be okay," I say and I place my hand on hers to reassure her. "Punch it."

She smiles softly and hits the pedal.

The engine makes noises nothing should ever make. Like a dying, asthmatic tyrannosaurus rex screaming one last scream while it claws furiously at a blackboard. But bless this little machine, it does not give up. Mary and I hold our breath. We don't speak or blink. We just hold hands and hope.

I see her lips moving and I know she's praying. All the jokes and snark that seem to define her are replaced by desperation but also, I can tell, by faith.

And then like the sun breaking the horizon and shattering the darkness we punch through the wall of the storm. And little by little we put some distance between ourselves and the tempest that had us in her guts only moments ago.

There's no sign of the drones. The storm ate them and has not, hopefully will not, let them go.

I see Mary breathe for the first time in a very long time.

"When we get inside the city," she says, "they won't chase us. You'll be much harder to spot with so many bodies around. Wait until you see the old girl. The city I mean. You're not going to believe it."

And she's definitely not wrong. The first thing I see is an enormous bubble of some kind around a city I do not recognize. Like someone placed a goldfish bowl upside down over a metropolis twenty times the size of Dubai.

"What in the—"

"The Terradome." she says.

"Terror dome?"

"Terra. Like Latin for "Earth." It's a combination of an arc generator, lasers, and microwaves. It keeps the storms out of the city. And UV rays. Heck, nobody would shoot one at us I don't think, but a nuke could bounce off that thing and nobody would even look up from their lunch. Allows us to control the weather and the temperature, too. We say when it rains and where and how much, now."

I'm too in awe of the thing to even ask questions. To me, it's the most amazing piece of engineering I've ever seen. For all I know, it doesn't crack the top thousand in this world. Where the heck even am I?

"You okay?"

"Yeah," I say. Just trying to wrap my head around it. "Do all cities have one of these?"

"A few do. But most cities are…not doing great. Climate change was…you guys should have cared a lot more about it."

Can't really argue with that.

"The UAE is doing well. Most of New Zealand. A couple of other places but a lot of the world is still in a pretty bad way."

We pass through a portal thing. Essentially a hole cut in the dome by some sort of stabilizing ring or something that allows cars in and out. And once we get inside we're not in a desert. We're in a…I don't even know. A savannah? A delta? It's green as far as the eye can see. I didn't know there could be this much green in all of the middle east.

I guess if you can control the weather you can grow just about anything any time. Amazing.

I gawk at it for a few minutes as the skyscrapers come closer and closer to us.

And then I remember something Mary said a little while ago. She told me to trust no one.

I cock my head a little to see if the speedometer is working again and it seems to be. We slowed down a ton once we got inside the dome. Now we've hit some traffic and slowed even more. We're only doing about fifteen kph.

The grass on the side of the road looks luscious and soft.

I quickly open the door and jump out.

She told me not to trust anyone and I don't. Including her.

Chapter 15

I hit pretty hard and roll to absorb as much of the impact as I can. I was right about the grass. It's softer than any ground I've ever felt. Like little green blades of pillows. I'm pretty sure nothing breaks.

It's thirty degrees cooler inside the bubble. The desert was hot and oppressive, as deserts tend to be. Now even though I'm outside and only a few meters away from the outside it feels like I'm in a movie theatre.

They went and air-conditioned a city.

In the distance, I hear brakes squealing. I hear Mary cursing in Chinese.

I get up and I do what detectives do best. I run. I hear Mary giving chase but she can't hope to catch me. She's no detective. And she was right, I do feel eighteen again. I feel like I could run forever.

I can't wrap my head around how this is remotely possible, but I'm heading into what looks to be a rainforest. A rainforest in Dubai.

Yesterday was a hundred years ago and I was chasing a fat old guy around for smoking money.

I don't suppose they still have cigarettes in the future.

Once inside the jungle, I take a hard left and climb a tree. A howler monkey had already staked out a branch of this thing and he looks at me like he wants to fight. I'm in the mood to oblige him, but first I need to be quiet.

I whisper at the little creature still staring me down,

"Don't start none there won't be none, monkey."

The monkey turns around and shows me its bottom.

Rude.

Mary is desperately searching for below. She has no clue where I am. It doesn't seem to occur to her to look up.

I don't know why she woke me from the fridge, I don't know why corporate compliance drones tried to re-kill me, I don't know anything about where and when I am. And I don't feel like taking chances.

There are too many variables, too many unknowns. Heck, almost literally everything here is unknown to me right now. I am a stranger in a strange land. I may as well be from Mars.

She can't search for long. Her car is stopped in the middle of a freeway.

"Khalifa!" she shouts in every direction. "Khalifa I wouldn't wake you up just to hurt you! The world needs you! Please come back!"

She waits a while. Shouts my name a while. Waits a little longer. I'm silent as a grave. Just me and my new monkey enemy who I will deal with soon.

She places a small piece of paper on a low branch of a banana tree about thirty meters away from me. "When you realize you need me too, call this number." And she walks away.

I wait another twenty minutes and I climb down.

As I descend, the monkey tries to hit me with some of its poo but it has terrible aim. "Suck it, monkey!" I yell back. I rip a mango off a nearby branch and hurl it at the monkey but my aim isn't much better.

I swear the dang thing sticks its tongue out at me before showing me its rear once again and climbing away.

I grab the card she left for me just in case, even though I don't have a phone, even though I don't even know if phones are still a thing, and make my way toward the city I've lived in my entire life and somehow also never met.

Along the way, I find about every fruit I've ever heard of and hundreds I haven't just sitting in trees and on bushes. Has to be hundreds of hectares of edible gardens surrounding the city. Nobody guarding it. No signs telling me not to touch. Just here for anyone to feast on I suppose. Which works out because I haven't actually eaten in about ten decades and I'm famished. I grab everything that looks good and I eat like I'm a teenager again, too.

I don't know if it's the future or starvation or what, but everything I put in my mouth is the best thing I've ever tasted.

It takes a few hours to get to the city proper. I grew up in the shadow of the Burj Khalifa, the tallest building in the world. It wouldn't reach the halfway point of any of the structures I see here. A toddler nipping at the heels of giants.

I don't know what I thought I'd find, but it isn't this. I guess I wanted Star Trek. Cars flying and people teleporting everywhere. Everyone wearing cool silver bodysuits. Maybe an alien or ten wandering around. Robot butlers at the very least I think.

I definitely expected to see an overpopulated, bustling crush of humanity on the streets but what I find feels like a pristine ghost town. An entire city that seems to basically be like one of those living rooms in rich people's houses that are so nice, so refined, so elegant that no one is actually allowed to live in it.

It's not even eight PM according to a clock outside what I think was a bank, but almost everyone seems to have retreated indoors. If they ever came out. The few people I do see stare at the ground as they move about and don't say a word to one another.

People cross the street or turn around and go the other way when they see me coming.

And everyone, every single person that I see, has a faint orange glow coming from their neck. Some kind of wearable tech I don't understand, I assume.

Everywhere there should be buskers or kids playing or workers wrestling away the stress of their jobs and wives and kids, there's just stillness.

It gets dark and the city becomes even more deserted The stars are wrong.

I used to lay under the stars for hours. By myself as a kid and later with Hanah. I memorized the sky. And it's wrong here.

I don't actually know what month it is, but it doesn't matter. There is no point during the year when these constellations appear in these places. Accounting for a century worth of drift doesn't make it make sense. It's like someone rearranged the heavens.

The terror dome. It must mess with the starlight. So they project their own night on the citizens. Most of whom, I'm guessing, don't leave the bubble. Ever. They chose the prettiest and most famous constellations and just put them where they thought they looked best, I guess.

It makes celestial navigation impossible here. How can you know where you are if you can't see the stars?

The moon has a logo on it for Allied Scientific Progress. The people who tried to kill us.

The goshdarn moon is a billboard.

That really can't be a good sign. But I try to put it out of mind. If I held a grudge against everyone who tried to kill me I'd never get anything done.

I walk for hours trying to get this city under my feet. Trying to understand what's happening here. Trying not to think about the fact that my parents and Afra everyone I ever cared about must have died forty years ago or more. I try not to think about the fact that more than any time in my ridiculous, cursed, dumb life I am completely alone. So I just keep walking.

Around hour five I find a cinema showing a midnight movie and I'm about to walk right past when I realize I've seen the poster in the window almost every day of my life.

Fury Fingers.

I slept in a coffin for a hundred years and when I woke up my father's movie, the worst movie ever made, is playing publicly. The film whose Rotten Tomato consensus is literally just "The most pointless ninety-three minutes in history", not only survived but found its audience? This makes no sense.

Darn right I trust no one and nothing.

It almost has to all be a dream, I think. But how would I know? How would I know if everything before this were also a dream? Maybe I'm just a brain bubbling in a vat in some mad scientist's lair with electrodes shocking me into thinking things.

Maybe. But if I am…so what? How would that change anything, really?

Maybe it's not a dream. Maybe this is not only real, it's a crucible.

There's a concept I learned about on a TV show once called "Post Traumatic Growth." Sometimes people who experience extreme trauma transform into entirely new individuals. And sometimes, maybe, they become exactly who they were always meant to be.

I don't know that I want to be anyone else, as much as I never much liked who I am. I also don't know that I have a choice at this point.

So I just keep walking.

I pass a swanky restaurant where, according to the banners on the wall and the forest fire on the cake, a lady seems to be celebrating her 145th birthday. She looks about sixty to my twenty-first-century eyes. I wind my way into a part of town like nothing I've ever seen. Every building seems to be a television. Dozens of two hundred story TVs in a single block that assaults my senses and pounds on my fight or flight response like no meth head with a gun or a knife ever has.

I see Buster Guff still selling something on one of the screens. Hilariously, he's selling Allied Scientific

Progress. He's behind the murder bots. It all sounds just about exactly right.

There's no way he's alive though, right? He was shilling self-driving cars and rocket rides and weed when I was in college. It's been a century. This is an old ad or a hologram or some nonsense, right? Like how Tupac keeps performing at Coachella despite being dead twenty years and how Fred Astaire danced with a vacuum in TV ads and things. Right?

But that lady at the restaurant a few blocks back was 145.

And Mary said something about different aging tech or something, didn't she?

And Buster was richer than rich. Crazy stupid rich. The laws of man never really applied to people with that kind of coin. Why should the laws of time here in this bonkers jungle of a future?

And then the worst thing that can happen to a crap magnet like me happens.

Hope.

I get absolutely clobbered upside the head by precious, audacious, poisonous hope.

Afra's family was pretty darn rich.

So I do what detectives do best. I run.

Chapter 16

The closer I get to the city center the more I start to recognize things. The city spread outward in every direction while I was napping. It tripled or maybe quintupled in size. The mad, beautiful dream of building a jewel in the desert kept growing. But the heart of the Dubai that I know is still beating, more or less, inside all of the new growth.

A lot of it has changed, been remodelled, and refurbished, and a lot of it has been preserved as historic landmarks. But I know where I am. For the first time since I woke up in the future, I'm not lost. At least geographically. And that's a start.

I take corners and turn down blind alleys so confidently I think, for a moment, I mostly forget I have no business being in the future.

And soon enough I'm standing at Afra's door. Or at least what used to be Afra's door, back when we were all definitely alive. Who knows whose door this is now. Hope springs, even where it never rains.

It doesn't look so different, really. There's clearly been an effort to preserve our people's history even as time and technology marched forward at terrifying speed.

The sun is just beginning to rise, though if it's actually the sun or just a projection of a burning ball of gas on the roof of a force field I do not know. Either way, I walked and ran and wandered all night.

I have no idea what's going to happen when I knock on this thing but if grifting car salesmen can survive a hundred years, surely the hardest, kindest lady left alive could. And if she's still alive, maybe she didn't move. Who on Earth in any century would sell property in downtown Dubai if they didn't have to? I look for a doorbell and I don't recognize anything. Then I realize that I don't see a handle or a lock, either. Even a door is beyond me, now. Walking into houses is too complex a task now.

So I knock.

From deep inside the home I hear a dog bark. Something small and cute that is utterly convinced it's fierce. A Shih Tzu I'd guess from the pitch of its growls. What's left of my cold, ragged heart leaps at the notion that dogs still exist. At least there's that.

As long as there are dogs there is love. And as long as there is love, we can make it I think.

Even the hardest, dumbest, most raggedy, and cynical hearts can never truly resist a puppy.

The door activates, I guess is the word, and basically transforms from stained wood into a three-meter tall TV. And my puppy-softened heart stops and my breath leaves me and my mouth goes dry. Because Afra is looking at me.

I try to speak but nothing comes out.

She just stares at me. Like she doesn't know me. Like she's wondering why this weird stranger is bothering her at sunrise. And that hurts worse than jumping from a moving car in the future. Surely a hundred years isn't enough time to forget a friend.

"What do you want? Speak quickly, the door is rigged to explode when people annoy me."

"It's me Afra," I say. "I know it's crazy but—" And then my keen detective eye notices Afra is maybe ten years younger than she was a hundred years ago. And there's a fleck of green in her brown eyes that wasn't there before. And her freckles have shifted a little. And this…isn't…Afra.

My heart sinks and breaks and all the voices in my worthless dummy head scream insults at me for thinking this could ever be a thing and I deserve their shame.

"Afra?" She says, confused but also like she's studying me. "Afra was my grandmother's name. Why would you be asking for…" she trails off, like she's caught something on the line but hasn't been able to reel it in just yet.

"Oh," I say. "I'm sorry. I was, well, I was cryogenically frozen a few decades ago if you can believe that which you probably can't, and I—" she cuts me off, thank goodness, because the labyrinth of that stuttering ramble was only going to get deeper, darker, and harder to escape.

"Oh my gosh! You're Khalifa. Khalifa bin Ahmed." And her face shifts from suspicion to something closer to amazement. Like she just saw a magic trick or a friendly ghost.

The look on my face must be pretty similar. Shock and awe. To say I'm amazed would be a severe understatement. I am blown away. I always said I wasn't even slightly interested in whether I was remembered once I was gone, but the idea that my name survived even a little inside this family that I loved, it means something. Something I'll probably need a lot of therapy to unpack. But I guess I've got time on my hands now. It's not like I have a job or a hobby if jobs and hobbies are even still a thing.

"Is she..." I have trouble asking because if the answer is 'no' this will all feel real and final and lost. "She's not still...?"

The young lady who is not Afra smiles softly and sadly. "No." She says. "She was killed in the line about a decade after you died. I didn't know her at all."

The door unlocks with a buzz and a click. "Why don't you come in for a coffee and we'll talk a little before I have to be at work?"

I smile and nod and head inside. If there is still coffee and dogs I may survive the new world after all.

The house looks the same and wildly different. The bones haven't changed, the layout hasn't changed, but of course, I've never seen any of this furniture. The art on the walls is different but old. Older, I think, than what Afra hung. It's all pop art from the fifties and sixties. Andy Warhol and Roy Lichtenstein and Keith Haring. It strikes me as odd that a young, modern woman would fancy this stuff, but I guess not that much crazier than people hanging renaissance stuff or Monet on their walls when I was growing up. Everything old is new again.

The young lady who is not Afra shows me to the kitchen and tells me her name is Moza. She offers some other standard, slightly awkward pleasantries, and she makes a coffee appear from a cabinet as if by magic.

She just whispered, "Two coffees, black, hot." And they showed up. It should be one of the craziest things I've ever seen and blow what little is left of my mind, but I'm too busy staring at the wall in astonishment. There's a poster of "Fury Fingers" in here. I recognize it. I gave it to Afra as a joke for her 25th birthday.

Moza notices me staring at it. "Your father's movie. Yes. That was my grandmother's and it's been passed down to me. Hard to believe a visionary like your dad only made one movie. He had so much more to give the world I think."

I choke on the really very good coffee when she says that. "A visionary? Everyone hated that thing. It's awful."

She smiles. "It was misunderstood in its time."

I shake it off. I want to know more about how that dumb movie that my lovely father made has become some kind of classic, but more than that I need to know about Afra. But even more than that I want a cigarette. Love and addiction.

"I know it's awful and probably insane to even ask but I don't suppose cigarettes survived the last hundred years?" I ask without really allowing myself to hope.

She laughs and heads back to the magic cabinet.

"Dare to dream, detective." She whispers to the cabinet "Twenty Cigarettes. Silk Cut. And a lighter." And when she opens the box there sits my salvation. I don't know if it's a teleporter or a maker like on Star Trek or what and right now I don't care.

She brings the pack over to me along with a plastic lighter. "They aren't taboo anymore. We beat cancer eighty years ago. Emphysema and most other things, too. One company made all the breakthroughs and changed the world. But you'll learn all about Allied Scientific Progress I'm sure."

"That name has definitely come up more than a few times in my short stay here," I say. I decide not to tell her they already tried to kill me a few times. Partly because I have no idea why they did that and partly because, as much as this young woman looks like my friend, she isn't. And I don't trust her. Not yet. "I'm sure," she says. "Pretty impossible to avoid them. But anyone can tell you about the corporation. Only a few people can tell you about my grandmother."

With her permission, I light the cigarette and inhale and hold to the smoke in my lungs like a life raft. I may never exhale again, I think.

Moza tells me she knows who I am because my death, or presumed death at least, was pretty famous. And because her grandmother left behind diaries. Journals with pictures and stories about me.

"I read all the case files you two closed together. You guys were quite a team."

I nod sadly at that. We were. We could have been more, maybe, if I hadn't been so lost and then so frozen. Metaphorically maybe before literally frozen.

Moza seems to read my mind. Her grandmother was intuitive, too. "I think you were the one she really wanted to be with, too," Moza says. "I hope that's not too forward. But you were married and then you were…well…she describes your life after your wife's murder in sparing detail."

"That was a kindness, I suppose."

"I thought I might have been." "I was a trainwreck. Still am, I guess. For me it wasn't a century ago, you understand."

She nods that she does understand.

"Was she…happy? Do you think? After I got fridged."

Moza thinks for a minute. "I don't know. She married a good man. She loved her daughter, my mom, fiercely. For the ten or so years she knew her. But she was haunted. She never let go of your murder. Or your wife's. She kept working it even though the killings stopped not long after you got hurt."

She empties some oranges from a bowl and slides the container in front of me to use as an ashtray. She tells me a few more stories from Afra's journals. The big moments she can remember off the top of her head from when she read them as a girl. We both laugh and I think we both try not to cry for the sake of the other. We talk for maybe twenty minutes. Three cigarettes. And then she glances at a watch on her wrist that seems to be a tattoo that tells the accurate time.

"I'd like to tell you more. I really would. But I'm afraid we're out of time."

And then she stands, unlocks a drawer with an ocular scan, and pulls out a gun.

I didn't see this coming.

Chapter 17

Moza is as intuitive as anyone I've ever known, I think. But I'm also pretty sure it doesn't take an empath to read me. I'm pretty shocked at the gun and the ease with which she handles it. And I have to actively fight to suppress my instincts. I've had enough guns pulled on me that a certain amount of muscle memory activates the seconds I see one in someone else's hands.

Am I scared? You have to care about being alive to be afraid of death, I think.

I'm not even angry, I don't think. I'm just really, really surprised. That's not an easy thing to do normally. But here in the new jungle, it seems to be my thing. The weapon isn't quite like the pistols I've always carried, there is a roundedness to it and a sleek cleanliness to the lines that's hard to describe. It's like if Apple made a handgun.

I've carried a weapon almost my entire life and never once been a fan of them. It's a tool to me. A necessary one sometimes. They've saved my life and a few other lives and they've cost me more than I'd like. But they are not something I've ever fetishized or worshiped like some of the nutbar PIs and all of the bat crap insane CSUs I've ever known.

Those nerds are great at what they do, but their brains are a bag of cats on the best days.

The point is, I don't love guns. But the thing in Moza's slender fingers I would definitely describe as "sexy." Moza laughs at the sight of me and slips the weapon into a holster I didn't clock under the jacket of her suit. "I'm a cop and I'm late for work is all I meant. Not that I'm going to murder you."

I laugh, too, but it's forced and I'm an awful actor. In school plays, I was always cast as a tree or a boulder or something. And frankly, I was pretty unqualified to play those roles.

"We haven't had a violent crime in Dubai in…I'd have to look it up. Ten years? Eleven?" she says, casting her eyes to the ceiling, trying to recall something from when she was maybe fourteen years old.

Maybe not in the city limits, I think. But some violence just went way the heck down outside the bubble. But I don't say that because it still feels dangerous to admit it to her.

"But you still carry guns?" I ask.

"This isn't a gun the way you think of them. Not like you carried. It these emit a burst of energy that essentially shuts down the human nervous system instantly. Puts you to sleep for the best rest you've ever had. Don't tell anyone, but I've actually popped myself with this little guy a couple of times when the insomnia got too much to bear."

Insomnia? I'm surprised these guys haven't wiped it out along with cancer and everything else.

"You like it? Being on the job?"

She wiggles her head in a motion that's not a nod or a shake. "I became a cop because I wanted to do good, like the grandmother I never met. Like you. Before the…well, before. But now that we know exactly who is exactly where at all times, and since we live in one nation under CCTV, and since most of the bad elements have been eradicated…I mostly help tourists find things. It's not the exciting life I've read about, but it's mine. And I'm sorry but I really have to get back to it."

I nod and stand up.

"Maybe," I say, "if it's not too much trouble, we could talk again some time. I've got Afra stories you wouldn't believe."

She smiles wide and brightly. "I'd love that." And she shows me to the door. And it's not until then that I notice it. Maybe I was too bewitched by how much she resembles my old partner, maybe it's the fact that I am fully overwhelmed by almost literally everything, but I didn't see it until she walked me out.

The back of her neck has a faint orange glow as well.

Back on the streets, Moza asks if she can drop me anywhere, but there's nowhere in this world that means anything more to me than anything else. There's nowhere I need to be and nothing I need to do. I'm nothing to anyone. Except maybe Mary. And what I am to her, I have no idea.

I take the card she left for me out of my pocket and stare at it for a few beats. And then I return it.

Maybe another time.

I'm starving again, but I don't have any money if money is even a thing in a world where you can whisper a brand of cigarettes into a cabinet and they appear.

The edible jungle is hours away by foot and I don't have any better ideas. So I decide I'm not that hungry after all. And that mostly works.

I think maybe I'll find a library. Try to catch up on a hundred years of human life. Shouldn't take more than an afternoon or two.

I have no idea where to find a library but surely I'll stumble onto one of them, or a helpful cop or something before too terribly long.

I only make it about three blocks before something flies into my path and hovers in front of me. Just parks itself right in my eye line and floats there.

It's small, blue, and rectangular. About the size of fifty or sixty dirham bills stacked on one another.

It speaks with a voice that I would describe as ninety-eight percent human. Not robotic like Siri or Alexa, but off enough that I know it's automated. The uncanny valley still hasn't quite been traversed, I think.

"Call for you," the floating thing says.

Nobody knows me to call me. And I don't have a number. Not anymore. So I don't say a word. I just step to the side.

The rectangle moves with me, blocking my path.

I step the other way and the rectangle moves again. "Urgent call for you, sir or madam or other. Please answer."

The last time I was this close to a flying drone it tried to shoot me a lot, so I'm not inclined to love this one, either.

I spin on my heel and head the other way. The rectangle rushes ahead of me and stops me in my path again. It's fast and it's nimble and now I really hate it. "Call declined," I say with more edge to my voice than I meant to muster.

"Unacceptable. Call is urgent. Please answer if convenient. If inconvenient, answer anyway." I swat at the thing like I'm King Kong taking out a Curtiss F8C Helldiver biplane atop the Empire State Building. But the little jerk is quick. Agile. I try to smack it again and again but nothing.

"Please say 'yes' to accept the call."

"No!"

"For the purposes of this call, 'no' will be treated as 'yes.'"

I wonder what that even means for the two nanoseconds I have before the box unfurls.

In just fractions of a second, it opens like an infinite greeting card, just unfolding time after time after time until it's bigger than me and on top of me and surrounding me.

And now I am inside the box and I'm not happy about it. It's dark and it smells too sterile.

I punch the wall and I think something in my little finger pops in a way bones are never meant to pop. The box is harder than me.

"Phone booths are extremely secure for your protection," the almost human voice says. "Call commencing in three, two, one."

One wall of the box turns on, much like Moza's door did, and a figure clad entirely in shadow is on the screen. I can only make out a silhouette.

"Hello, detective," it says. "Very nice to see you again." His voice is being altered. Obscured. Instead of being a robot trying to sound human, it's a human trying to mask his voice with robotics.

"Who is this? I just stopped being dead and I am not in a gaming mood!"

"I understand you must be upset and overwhelmed. Frankly, this is all a surprise to me, too. I'll explain everything but—"

"Explain it now!"

"This line is not secure, kyah. I need you to trust me."

Kyah? Well how about that. I don't know how and I don't know why, but I know exactly who I'm talking to. Or at least I know who someone wants me to think I'm talking to. That brings a smile to my face despite everything.

The shadowy figure can see on my face that I recognize him and that I'm happy about it.

"Don't say my name. Just come to this place and let's have some food with me. You must be famished. I know I am."

A small piece of paper prints from a slot on one wall of the phone booth.

"How do I know this isn't a trick? Because that seems more likely than this being real if you know what I mean."

"I do know what you mean. But I also know you don't have much choice. Where you gonna sleep? Where you gonna eat? And more importantly, why are you going to keep going? I've got food and beds and oh man do I have a purpose for you, kyah. And if I'm lying, you get to be dead which is I think what you really want anyway. It's win/win for you."

I can't help but smile at that, too. It's nice when people get me.

I look down at the paper that came from the wall and it's not an address. It's not exactly nonsense, but it's not exactly sense either.

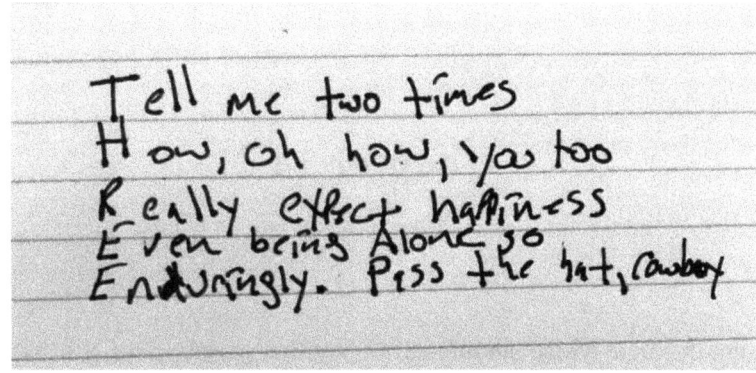

"What is this?" I ask. "This isn't an address?"

"Isn't it? Line isn't secure, brother. But you'll see it when you see it. And then I'll see you again."

And the screen goes dead. And the box folds back up on itself until it is again a little bigger than a wallet.

"Thank you for using A-S-P mobile for your private phone call needs. And thank you for keeping your pants on the entire time."

I try to smack the little blue box one more time for good measure and of course, I miss. But this time it flies away into the distance and I pretend it was scared of me which does make me feel just a little better.

And I'm left with just this note that makes no sense.

I really do hate the future.

Chapter 18

So I've got this note which amounts to yet another puzzle in my life and oh boy do I hate puzzles.

It's a cipher, I suppose. A code. Unless it's just a weird poem and he's messing with me which is entirely possible. I also hate poems.

But let's assume it's a cipher. It's an age-old way to pass secret messages when you know they can be intercepted.

The first thing to do when someone gives you a coded message like this is to get really mad about it. Swear a bunch and maybe do some growling. Growling helps.

Maybe my most famous arrest back when I was a cop was a guy who went by the name Saahir the Sublime. He was a failed magician who apparently decided to just go on ahead and become a Batman villain. He'd rob high-end jewelry shops and museums and things wearing his magician outfit, the tophat, the tails, carrying a magic wand, the whole deal. He'd use all the cunning trickery he learned for his act to nick diamonds and watches and dinosaur bones and things.

And the most maddening thing about him was that he was good at it.

He literally stole an entire stegosaurus one time. He did it piece by piece, one bone every few days, replacing the real fossils with plaster moulds he'd made in a creepy workshop. It took him months.

He was so good, in fact, that nobody noticed his first several crimes even happened for days or weeks. Even the dinosaur nobody noticed because he replaced each piece perfectly. And when they did eventually realize something was stolen, nobody really talked about it because the whole thing was so mysterious and or embarrassing. Like the stuff just vanished. Employees were questioned and insurance scams were suspected because it was all so clean it had to be an inside job. And those sorts of things just aren't sexy or fun. So nobody talks about them.

And Saahir wanted to be talked about.

You don't name yourself "the Sublime" because you want to blend in with the crowd.

So he got bolder. He started making sure we knew it was him. He started leaving riddles and codes and things to tell us what he'd rob next.

And still, nobody much cared. Things get stolen every day and people are weird every day and a few million in jewelry and a Jurassic lizard aren't the headline grabbers they once were.

So Saahir the Sublime started killing people.

The note on the first body he left, found after an armoured car robbery, was written in blood. Because Saahir was dramatic. It read, "What can go up a chimney down, but can't go down a chimney up?"

The powers that be gave it to me at that point because the magician had escalated to dropping bodies. And because I hate puzzles and the world hates me.

Saahir got away with a few million in cash that day. I cared way more about the son who didn't have a father anymore.

The murder was grizzly and left no physical evidence. He melted the guard's face and neck with fluoroantimonic acid. Saahir tricked the poor guy into drinking it with his Red Zinger hibiscus tea.

The acid ate right through the guy's chin and his tongue and his windpipe. He could breathe in through the holes in his neck for a little while, the medical examiner said. It would have taken some time for the end to come. A good man who worked for a living and was raising a son on his own died gasping. Just so someone would pay attention to pitiful little Saahir.

So I paid attention.

I stared at that note for hours just trying to make sense of the language before something clicked for me. Eventually, I realized that if I strip away the weird wording one could ask the same question like, "What is too big to fit in a small space when it's what we would call 'up' but not when it's what we would call 'down?'" And that made sense somehow. The answer is "an umbrella."

Now that solution could lead to a lot of things, but at the time the Dubai Mall was pretty famous for having an entire ceiling covered in colorful umbrellas. So I reasoned he'd rob the mall. But it's a pretty big building. More than 1,200 shops spread over a total floor area of 5.9 million square feet. So we posted as many men as we could there and it didn't matter. He didn't rob the stores.

A little after two P.M. on the following Wednesday, lightning crashed inside the building electrocuting half a dozen people who were sitting on a fountain. They boiled from the inside, I'm told. Their skin blackened like chicken left too long in the fryer. Six people gone in a flash so some jackass could get his name on the news.

Then it started to rain right there in the food court. And while nobody was looking, because they were too busy dying or screaming or both, he didn't bother to rob a store. He stole every one of the umbrellas. About a thousand umbrellas just *poof* gone.

They weren't valuable or anything. He just did it because he could. Because people would talk about it.

In place of the umbrellas, he left a note that said, "I have branches, but no fruit, trunk, or leaves. What am I?" That riddle any child could crack. The answer is "a bank."

Of course, there are hundreds of banks in a city with the size and wealth of Dubai. There's no way to police them all. No way to even begin.

But my guy was too clever by half. He wrote the note on a torn piece of sheet music. No lyrics, no title or attribution, just the notes on the scale.

The dots and lines on the page may as well have been hieroglyphics for all they meant to me, so I took it to a friend of mine who plays guitar like some kind of rock and roll angel.

He said he didn't recognize it offhand, but he could play it. He could play anything.

He strapped on his ax, a Fender Jag-Stang modelled after the one made specifically for Kurt Cobain, and he played what few notes we could see on the page. And even though it only amounted to a few seconds of music, it was enough. We both recognized it immediately. The song was "03 Bonnie & Clyde" by Jay-Z featuring Beyoncé.

Cute, right? Because Bonnie and Clyde were pretty famous American bank robbers from the 20th century. They made a couple of movies about them over the years and everything. The bank robber left us a note referencing some bank robbers.

But that was a head-fake. That was the misdirection. The magician getting you to look at the pretty girl while he switches out the real sword for a fake one. Lucky for me, I'm not just a fan of good music, I'm also a sports fan.

The real clue was Jay-Z.

I started asking myself what I knew about him, and it was quite a lot, I was surprised to find. I knew ten or fifteen of his songs by heart. I knew he was born with the name Shawn Carter. I knew he was a drug dealer before he became the de facto poet laureate of America for a while. I knew he was married to maybe the hottest and most successful woman in the world and that still wasn't enough to keep him from cheating on her, apparently. I knew about "Becky with the good hair."

And I knew Jay-Z liked sports, too.

He notably bragged in one of his songs that he "made a Yankee cap more famous than a Yankee can." But more importantly for my purposes, he liked the NBA. A lot. Enough to buy into it.

At that time he was part owner of a basketball team in the U.S. called "The Brooklyn Nets." And where do the Nets play? In an arena Jay-Z also partially owned called "The Barclays Center."

Barclays is a bank headquartered in London. Or it was. Who knows if they're still around. But they were a big one back then. They did about twenty-two billion a year in revenue when I was alive the first time 'round. And they only had one branch in Dubai.

One single branch was a thing I could definitely police. No problem.

The brass weren't as convinced I was right as I was, but they gave me three officers for a week to try to bring the monster down. We set up in the Barclays every day and on the fifth day my man Saahir the Sublime appeared in a puff of smoke. Just *poof* there he was right under the crystal chandelier.

He laughed the laugh of a man of certainty. The laugh of a murderer who knew for sure he was going to kill again and get away with it and be famous for it.

And he began his performance.

I let him get almost six words out before I shot him with a taser.

When he was on the ground I shot him with a second taser just because I hated that guy. He urinated all over himself and then it was my turn to laugh.

This time the plan was to release party balloons filled with mustard gas after he'd left. He'd have killed thirty people that day at least. They would have died in agony. For a show. For a pitiful creature's tattered ego.

I got my photo in a lot of papers after that. Got a handshake from some really important people who forgot my name before they let go of my hand. I think they gave me a medal or something.

Saahir the Sublime went away for a few lifetimes. *Poof*, you're in jail forever! But he never did tell me what he did with all those umbrellas. And, honestly, that still eats at me a little.

Anyway, the point is, I hate puzzles.

And I hate ciphers even more than puzzles.

My friends, back when I had friends, liked to do escape rooms sometimes. For fun. Where you go and solve a bunch of cryptograms and unlock boxes and cryptexes and defuse fake bombs and things. I never went along. I've felt like I needed to escape from basically every room I've ever been in. Why would I pay for it?

But I don't have anything better to do right now. And much more importantly I'm pretty sure I know who was on the other end of that call. And if I'm right, I really do want to talk to him. So let's do this.

Tell me two times

How, oh how, you too

Really expect happiness

Even being alone so

Enduringly. Pass the hat, cowboy

Yeah. Okay. So first things first is it doesn't make any literal sense. At least none that I can find. How do I expect to find happiness? I don't.

Even if I did, there are too many possible answers. The solution has to be a single, definite thing. A thing that leads me somewhere.

Most likely, this code was made just for me. And the person knows me at least a little. So it could be something personal. Something tailored just for me.

But if it is, I don't see it. Nobody ever called me "cowboy." I've never even seen a cow that wasn't in a movie or on a bun or a plate I don't think.

Why would I tell him twice? Maybe the answer is a word or phrase that's the same thing repeated? Something like "tut tut," "hear hear," "chop chop," or "knock knock." Knock knock? Maybe it's all a joke? "Knock knock."

"Who's there? A sad, angry detective. A sad, angry detective who?" Maybe. This doesn't feel like anything. So I work the problem. Start from the outside in this time.

The most common codes you see out in the wild, I think, are substitution ciphers. Where one letter always stands in for another. "E" is really a "B" and "K" is really "L" and so on.

So "EKPN" is really "BLUE." It's just about figuring out what is standing in for what. You used to see these kinds of ciphers in the newspaper puzzle section a lot back when there were newspapers. But those codes pretty much always appear as nonsense until they're solved. Not as recognizable words and even sentences.

The sentences in this note may be dumb, but they just about make sense. Sort of. If you squint a little and stand on your head and maybe hold it up to a mirror.

Every entry in every high school literary journal is worse, let's put it that way.

Wait! Hold it up to a mirror. Maybe. Maybe something is revealed when I see it reversed.

I walk until I find something shiny enough to get a good reflection. It doesn't take long. I find a shop whose windows are TVs or screens of some kind. It's playing news from around the world.

Mass graves in a soccer stadium in Brazil, the bodies piled to the nosebleed section. It doesn't say why.

A war in Greenland being fought with sticks and stones. They ran out of bullets and bombs years ago, I guess, and now they're just slashing and tearing at one another with whatever they can find. It's savage. Feral. Like something out of a zombie movie. Only there are no survivors. It's zombies all the way down now. Even small children are bashing one another with tree branches for something, it doesn't say what. It doesn't say why they're fighting or who's winning. How could anyone be winning this? It doesn't say how mankind can get to a state like this.

There's a shot of Japan. Each of the islands is just a steel dome now. What's underneath is anyone's guess. The TV says it's day 8,321 since anyone went in or anyone came out. They could all be dead for all the world knows. Or it could be one big theme park in there.

I don't recognize this world at all. As awful as it was when I left…this is so much worse. At least everything on the screens is.

But then there's Dubai. My home. Where they made a rainforest in a desert and the streets are sparkling clean and Afra…I mean Moza…says there hasn't been a violent crime in living memory.

I can't wrestle with all that right now. Right now there is only the puzzle.

I hold the note up to the shiniest part of the window and it's a good mirror. I can read it easily. And what I read is:

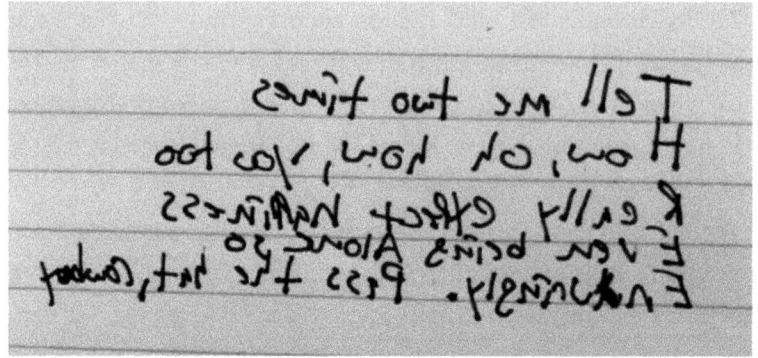

I stare at it for long enough that four people see me gawking at my reflection, turn, and run away.

Yeah. This is officially nothing. I was hoping an image or a pattern or something would pop out. But it really is just some weird words backward.

Have I mentioned I hate puzzles?

Work the problem, detective. What's next?

Shift ciphers are also very common with secret messages. That's where you just slide up or down the alphabet a bit for each letter in a code. Shift thirteen letters forward, for example, and "One for all and all for one" becomes "Bar sbe nyy naq nyy sbe bar." Because "B" is thirteen forward from "O" and "A" is thirteen forward from "N" and so on.

As long as you know how much to shift and in which direction, they're easy to solve. Even if you don't know what the key is, with computers they're super easy to brute force because even a fifteen-year-old phone can try every rotation possibility in the time it takes you to notice the page refreshed.

But then again you have the nonsense factor. Those codes aren't readable as anything until they're solved.

I think they also call that a Caesar cipher because one of the Roman emperors used it back when you couldn't break it in nanoseconds with a machine.

In fact, that's the whole point, isn't it? The call inside that awful blue box was being monitored. If someone or something intercepted that, they'd plug it into a program and crack it like an egg instantly. So it has to be a code a computer can't easily break. It has to be something that would require a human to solve. That eliminates a ton of options.

And it's meant to give me an address. Someplace to meet him. So maybe we can work backward by looking for common street names or a business or an intersection or something. Maybe GPS coordinates.

My mind feels like it's moving at speed now. Maybe for the first time since I got to the future. This feels like a way forward.

But it's just a starting point. If that's all I have to go on, getting confused and turned around could be super easy. "Cowboy" for example, could point to a country western bar, or "Ranch Street" if that's a thing that exists or a hundred other things.

So what else? Look for the oddities. He must have left some kind of map that would let me untangle this thing. A key to unlock the puzzle box.

The line breaks are weird. Nobody would write like this unless it's a clue or they're having a stroke or something. And strokes probably don't happen anymore. At least not in this city, I'd imagine.

There are five lines. What does five mean? What comes in fives? Five fingers per hand. Five toes per foot. What else comes in fives? Jacksons. Spice Girls, I think. There are five vowels in the English language. Maybe I only read the vowels? No, that's insane. Consonants are pretty important.

"E" is the fifth letter of the English language. It's also the most common letter. If I read only the words that contain the letter "E" I get: Tell me times

Really expect happiness

Even being alone

Enduringly. the

And…that's nothing. Maybe it's not something to do with fives after all. What else do we know for sure about the thing?

The note contains twenty-one words in total. What does that get us? That's the legal drinking age in some countries. Another name for the card game Blackjack, where the goal is to collect cards that reach but do not exceed twenty-one. It was probably a gamble to contact me but…I'm not seeing it.

Twenty-one total words. Five lines. Twenty-one divided by five is four-point…something. I don't know. I can't do that math exactly.

If I read only the first word of every line I get, "Tell How Really Even Enduringly." Nothing.

Man oh man do I hate puzzles.

I'm hours in and I'm nowhere. But something gnaws on me in the back of my skull telling me that I'm nearing something important. It's the detective's intuition or my gut or I've got a guardian angel or something, I don't know. But ever since I was a little kid I can almost always tell when something is about to make sense. I get a little tingle that says, "Pay attention. You're close." And I've got that tingle right now.

It could be a skip code! Five lines is the key! I'm meant to read every fifth word to get the message. That would make the real message, "How really alone hat."

What?

More nonsense and more dead ends. Hello, Square One. Nice to see you again. So much for the tingle, ya daft detective.

I pocket the note and walk a little more. Just in circles.

Just lost. I hear birds but I don't see any. I wonder briefly if birds are still a thing. Or if they just pump in the sounds of birds throughout the city to make people feel like the world isn't going extinct around them. Fake birds like the fake stars that didn't make sense last night. I don't know. But monkeys are still around, I know that for sure, so I hold out hope for the birds. And I hope they're not as mean as monkeys.

Nothing pops for me as I wander so I sit under a tree that's both older than me and also hadn't yet been planted when I crashed my first car on this street on my seventeenth birthday. I was swerving to avoid a cat. The cat lived. My Chrysler Le Baron did not.

I take the note from my pocket and I stare at the paper trying to will it into coherence. Like if I just want it enough the thing will take pity on me and start making sense.

I turn it upside down. Hold it up to the light to try to read it backward but not mirrored. When I do that the message becomes:

Cowboy hat the pass enduringly.

So alone being even

Happiness expect really

To you, how oh, how

Times two me tell

Honestly, that makes about as much sense as reading it forward. But nothing cracks for me except my patience.

I pace a bit. Sit a bit. Lie down in some more of that ridiculously nice grass they got here. Who knew grass technology had so much left to give us?

I don't know how late it is, but judging by the sun it's gotta be two or three o'clock by now. That means I've been at it for hours and—Three!

It's an epiphany like you mean it. Just like that, I see it staring me in my dumb face. The answer is screaming through the fog and I may start dancing right here in these beautiful, deserted streets.

It *is* about the line breaks. And it *is* a skip code. I knew the detective tingle wouldn't let me down!

I was close, but I was missing the key. It's an acrostic, too. The first letter of each line spells THREE. I am meant to read every third word.

"Two oh too happiness alone pass cowboy."

I did it. I know for sure I did. I broke it before it broke me. Maybe just before. I made it make sense. It only looks like gibberish if you don't know the city. I know exactly where I'm going.

Chapter 19

In 2017, which was somehow both a couple of years and a century ago, a main street in The Dubai International Financial Centre was renamed
"Happiness Street."

It was done to coincide with The International Day of Happiness, which was a made-up holiday established in 2012. I guess all holidays are made up after a fashion, but this one seems extra made up. Or maybe it just feels that way to me because I'm a miserable son of a gun.

The holiday was created by the United Nations General Assembly to make people around the world realize the importance of happiness in their lives. Because nothing says joy like the UN General Assembly.

And suddenly I find myself wondering if the UN still exists in the far-flung future. And then I remember that I don't really care.

Anyway, they went and named a street "Happiness."

A few years later Happiness Street, which stretched along the Dubai World Trade Centre from Emirates Towers to the Burj Khalifa district, was renamed Mustaqbal Street.

And Mustaqbal Street, which was until then near City Walk, was renamed Happiness Street. It played merry Hell with navigation software for a while, but people can adapt to just about anything.

That's the street I was sent to by the note. And "two oh too" is just 202 spelled out to confused dumb robots. It was a street address, just like the shadowy figure said. "Mustaqbal," by the way, means "future" in Arabic. So my friend is really having quite a laugh at me, I think. He is clever, I'll give him that.

It doesn't take too long to get to Happiness on foot from Moza's place. The streets aren't much more alive with people now than they were last night. And in the daylight, I can see how slight everyone looks. Frail, almost. And scared of their shadows. It may take a lifetime to come to know this new homeland of mine.

If I didn't know better I'd guess they were all sick to the point of near-death and malnourished. But food grows all over the place for anyone to grab. Magic cabinets make anything you might want to eat appear, I think. And the corporation that tried to kill me for no reason has apparently wiped out disease.

Of the seven people I pass on my walk, every single one either crosses the street or runs away. Not one looks me in the eye.

And they all have the orange light on their necks.

On the way I pass several more buildings whose entire exterior appear to be television screens. All showing AS-P news, which is basically always a horror show that would have fetched an R or maybe an NC-17 rating in my day.

Australia has become a wasteland. Global warming almost literally boiled off all the potable water there, it seems. Most people either died of thirst or were killed in the Water Wars. And the ones that are left are still fighting over drops of H2O. The population of the entire continent is thought to be less than a thousand now. Nobody knows for sure because no journalist has visited in the last forty years and come back alive. Drone footage shows no crops and no animals left to hunt or farm. The unlucky few who survived are almost certainly eating each other.

The Koreas just went ahead and blew themselves up with nuclear firepower of a few hundred stars. Both countries are just smoking, radioactive holes in the ground, more or less. No survivors. Experts think those areas may be habitable again in one thousand years.

There's apparently a moon colony now. A moon city seems more like it. At the very least a moon downtown with several skyscrapers and a small suburb. Things up there seem to be going great. The crops are flourishing, people are happy and content, their soccer team just won the World Cup. Most of the Earth seems to be absolutely on fire, metaphorically and literally, but people will always find a way to play football.

The United States appears to no longer be united or made of states. It seems like it's about five smaller countries now, each with huge, ugly walls guarding their borders. The South, as it's now known as a sovereign nation, has created mutants, I think is the only word for it. Genetic testing trying to combine human and animal DNA has gone about as well as movies and TV would lead you to believe it would. Halfbear people are ripping the heads right off of half-deer people and eating them in the husk of downtown Atlanta. Half-cats fight half-wolves for control of Nashville. And those are the success stories. Most of the results were just crippled, crumpled things with feathers and tails that lived for a few moments in agony before begging for death. I can't help but wonder if that country has a soccer team. The darkest parts of me do want to see them play.

I try to take in as much of it as I can, but none of it feels real to me. It's probably like the old story of the frog in the boiling water. The citizens of the world today, they saw all this happen gradually and it's just the way things are. For me I've been thrown right into the pot already at a rolling boil. And I want to jump the heck out in a hurry. I want to do what I do best and run.

But I press on. Because what else am I going to do, honestly?

When I make it to my destination, what I find can't help but make me smile. It's a soul food restaurant called "Have A Nice Day Cafe." It's painted bright blue with big yellow smiley faces all over the place. Even the door pulls are smiley faces. It seems so out of place in this world. And so do I.

I walk in and the place is straight out of the fifties or something. Like an old diner you'd see on reruns of "Happy Days" or "Alice" or something.

The large man behind the counter doesn't appear to be having a nice day. In fact, he doesn't look to me like he's ever had a single nice day. He glares at me and not for the first time since waking up in the future I feel naked without a gun.

"What?" he spits at me. Not exactly service with a smile in whatever century this is.

It's jarring because he's not only the first person other than Moza and Mary to talk to me, he's the first one to not run away from me on sight. And he's the first one that doesn't look like they could slip down a shower drain never to be heard from again. It would take a mighty drain to put this monster in danger. A sinkhole would be scared of him.

I came to where the note told me to go. I came alone as the note told me. The only thing left is the password the note gave me.

"Cowboy," I say confidently.

The man behind the counter gives me a slight nod and says, "Yippee-ki-yay."

He types a few things into the ancient cash register with lightning-quick fingers and the entire floor disappears beneath my feet. Just *ZIP* the whole thing is gone in an instant.

Guess I was wrong about who brought me here.

Guess it *was* a trap.

I fall.

I fall through blacker-than-pitch darkness.

I fall for longer than should be possible. Six seconds? Ten? Long enough that I must have reached terminal velocity. Long enough that there's virtually no way I don't die when I hit the ground. Heck, I'm not just going to die, I'm going to splatter. Like a melon dropped on concrete. Even if there's, like, a pool of water down there I'm dead.

I make my peace with it. Maybe I'm even excited about it.

Maybe. A little.

Maybe I get to see my parents again. And Hanah. And Afra. And Humaid. Maybe.

I close my eyes and I hope I remember how to say a quick prayer. To my surprise and delight, I do. And I wait for the end. And I hope it won't hurt. And I know I probably deserve it if it does.

And I fall a little more.

And then I just…don't die.

I slow to a stop like I was caught by gentle hands and lowered to the ground. And I can breathe. I'm on my feet again and whatever held me has let me go. Some kind of tractor beam or something.

I wrestle with the disappointment of still being alive for just a moment before I focus on trying to sort out what the heck is happening.

And the room is still completely dark.

And I hear a laugh like rolling thunder. Not a menacing thing. A double-barrel shotgun blast of joy that echoes around the cavernous room and fills me from the bones out.

For once, I actually wasn't wrong.

I just can't ever seem to help myself. Even after he pulls a stunt like that, I like this guy.

"Come on out, Manny," I say a little louder than maybe was necessary.

A light flips on illuminating a big, weird space and there he is. Not as massive as when I knew him. Somehow bigger. He's a battleship of a man with the guns to sink an entire navy and not one inch of him below the chin isn't covered in elaborate tattoos.

He's aged but not a hundred years. Maybe twenty?

And I kid you not, my guy Manny is sitting on a freaking throne. A dark, Brobdingnagian piece of oak, maybe, or maybe pine, studded with gold skulls with ruby eyes. It's as subtle as everything else about this dude that I swear you cannot help but like.

"Khalifa, kyah! How the heck are you?"

"Kyah" is slang for "older brother" in Tagalog. Am I still the older brother?

My keen detective brain starts putting some things together. Who had the money to freeze me back in the day? Who had the stones to wake me even though it's apparently bananas illegal? Who, in this future where everything is different and cold could still be the same and warm and perfectly himself? Of course, it was Manny all along.

"Mary is your daughter. I just got that."

Another explosive laugh. "A brilliant, impetuous, beautiful outlaw. That acorn didn't fall far from the tree, huh?"

"No sir," I say. "It's good to see you, big guy. I have a million questions. For starters."

"It would be wild if you didn't!"

"I guess the most pressing one is this, why did you wake me up?"

"I didn't, brother."

Mary steps into the light. She got gorgeouser. "I did," she purrs. I actively try to stop myself from falling in love. I'm successful ish.

"Frankly if I'd known what she was up to I never would have let her do it. I'd have locked her in a tower and thrown away the key. No offense." I shake my head. I really don't take any.

"She's tricky, though. And whip-smart. She's a problem solver, kyah. So she took matters into her own hands, for better or worse. And I pray it isn't worse. She only saw one solution to the biggest problem of the last century." "Me?" I ask Mary.

"You," she says with a smile that's more of an apology than anything else.

"Why?"

"The serpent cult," she says. "They're killing again." Of course they are.

"And you're our Obi Wan, detective. You're our only hope."

Of course I am.

Chapter 20

Part of me can't believe after a hundred-year nap I still have to deal with these monsters. And part of me is kind of glad I still have a shot at some kind of revenge. Whoever killed my wife and my brother is long dead, but I can hammer some kind of vengeance into their descendants. And that might help me sleep a little better I suppose.

"I need to know oh so many things," I say to Manny,

"but my next question has to be how are you still alive?"

"I'm not, brother." He says with a chuckle. "At least not how you probably mean it." And I'm lost. Which I guess I'm at least kind of getting used to at this point. "Am I at a seance or something?"

Manny snaps his fingers and he disappears. Just gone in a blink.

Then I hear his voice behind me say, "Boo!"

I jump so far out of my skin that I swear I can see my meat suit beneath me. He scared me onto the astral plane for a second.

Manny laughs harder than I've ever heard him laugh, which is saying more than a little, while I try to will my heart into slowing down from the one-trillion beats per minute it's currently going at. "He loves doing that," Mary says.

"Why? And how?"

"The singularity, brother. It's insanely illegal and costs more than a good-sized country to pull off, but I fully merged my consciousness with machines before they got me. I'm currently talking to you as a hologram. But I have a pretty sweet robot body I can control, too, for a more hands-on experience. It's still got some kinks to work out of that guy, though. Last time I shook hands with a bro I accidentally snapped a few fingers right off." I gag a little at the thought. "We can grow those back now! Not as bad as it could be! But I figured being new and all you'd rather keep all your parts."

"You really are a genius."

I reach out my hand and it passes right through him. Like he's a ghost. It is very weird.

I ask them to tell me about the serpent cult and together Manny and Mary fill me in on a hundred years of horror.

First of all, they say, my death or near-death I guess, was pretty famous at the time. I was the subject of a few documentaries and roughly one thousand true crime podcasts. Not because I'm that interesting but because I exposed the tip of one part of a murderous cult that, most people think, has been active since prehistory. They've been killing people for thousands of years, tens of thousands, and nobody even really noticed.

To ratchet up a body count like they have without drawing the kind of attention genocide usually gets may be the scariest thing I've learned about them yet. That shows not just skill through the ages, but an ability to manipulate levers of power most people can't begin to imagine even existing.

They started in China sometime before we started counting years maybe. No one has ever been caught or admitted to being a part of the organization. Not one loud mouth drunk or memoirist who just couldn't stand not getting the credit for the horror they caused in all that time. They are known only by their trail of dead.

They kill in twelve-year cycles, only in the years of the snake according to the Chinese zodiac. And wouldn't you know it, this year happens to be one of those years. And Chinese New Year was last week. There have already been more than two hundred deaths that fit their M.O. Mary thinks. None of them in the UAE. They seem to have multiple hunting grounds, but this isn't one anymore. At least not yet.

When I exposed them it was the closest anyone has come to catching one. There was actual evidence. There were bodies they couldn't get rid of in time. The ones I gunned down.

And there were weapons

Hidden in the walls of that room were 1,104 blades. Each one identical. Each one still stained with the blood of a separate unsolved murder victim. 1,104 blades, 1,104 dead men and women that nobody even thought of trying to connect. Bodies on every inch of the globe. And each blade was dipped in venom. The venom of the Inland taipan to be exact. The deadliest snake in the world.

Anything worth doing is worth doing right, I guess.

News media and true crime fanatics across the globe went nuts for the story for a while. A thousand armchair detectives spun a thousand different theories but nobody ever found anything else ever again. And the killings stopped at the end of the year of the serpent.

And the world moved on.

Though the car I stole that day is apparently still on display in a crime museum uptown. My blood is still all over it and everything, they say. A lovely thought.

When the killings started again twelve years later, people had moved on to new crime stories and once again no one connected the dots and they did their work in obscurity again. And maybe that's the evil genius of their scheme. Nobody can maintain outrage or interest for more than a decade, even in mass murder I guess.

At least most people can't.

Afra kept digging and digging the whole time. Manny helped as best he could. They made a formidable team, but they were up against something the world has never seen. Or never knew they were seeing, at least. Billions of dollars, a global network stretching back thousands of years, the illogical, unstoppable devotion of cultists, true evil genius at the head of the snake, once assumes…it was too much for any two people. Even these amazing ones.

They got beat.

In 2037, the next year of the snake after I was shuffled into the fridge, Afra was killed at ten AM on February 15. Chinese New Year. They didn't waste one single day.

For the rest of the world, she's a ghost. A distant memory if anything at all. For them, she's been gone for ninety years. For me, it's brand new and I struggle to contain my rage and sorrow. And a big part of me wants to run. It is, after all, what I'm best at.

I remind myself there will be time to mourn after I've hit all the people that need hitting until my hands bleed and shatter and snap off. I'll get Manny to grow them back and then I'll hit more people until they break off again.

Manny can see me fighting back the surges of fury. "I know it's a lot, bro," he says. "We can take it slow. You want a kebab or ten? Mary, get this man some kebabs please. We make great kebabs here. I've had a century to perfect the recipe, bro."

Mary nods and heads off. I'm too angry to eat but I'm also too angry to argue.

"You want, like, a nap?" he asks with real concern in his voice. "Or a massage? My guy Sven is a miracle worker. Or I can—"

"I want to keep going."

"Yeah, bro. Of course. So I got pretty rich. And by 'pretty' I mean 'insanely.' I invented a few new kinds of AI. And a bunch of other stuff. At one point I just started watching sci-fi movies and seeing what I could make real. I made most of it, kyah! And the Terradome? That was me. Pretty cool, right? Anyway. I spent unholy amounts of that money trying to stop these monsters from killing other people. And even more money trying to stop them from killing me. I ran them to ground a few times, I think. I had a team of a couple hundred detectives and mercenaries closing in on them at one point." Manny gets quiet like you mean it for a bit. "They all died. I got them all dead."

I don't know what to say so I say, "I'm sorry, man. I'd hug you if I could."

"Want me to get the Manny-bot?"

"No!" I yell with visions of my spine ripped from my body and turned to jello.

Manny laughs again and he's back to his old self. It's like he can flip a switch. And not for the first time, I am jealous of him.

"I almost had them at least a couple of times. And then one day they had me," he says wistfully. "I still don't really know how they did it. How they got past my security and whatnot. I just woke up dead, basically. But the autopsy confirmed snake venom in my blood. Some people thought they put it in my food, but that doesn't track."

"Your stomach acids would have killed the venom," I say.

"Exactly, brother. And my chef was a good guy."

"When this is all done and I've beaten them, and I will beat them," I say, "we're going to find out that a lot of people we thought were good guys were, in fact, monsters."

Manny nods. "The dudes you killed in that room that day, the ones in the snake masks, they were CEOs and little league coaches and stuff. Good people everyone thought. So…yeah. I'm thinking you're right on that one, kyah."

"I hate that I never got to see that room," I say. "I mean with the walls exposed. The weapons. Maybe I could have seen something nobody else saw."

"You wanna see it? Here you go."

And the dark dungeon throne room I was standing in immediately transforms. In a flash, I'm standing in that bright, barren room in the basement of the hotel. I see the men I killed still bloody and dead on the floor. And I see the knives adorning the place.

They aren't just hung on the walls, they're arranged in patterns. Intricate designs. Constellations of death. It's not just decoration, it's a story. I don't know how to read it, yet. But I can tell that it's a tale. It's information. And that someone was proud of it. The blades are a tapestry telling the history of these kills. It's the most horrific thing I've ever seen.

"I had it recreated down to the dust patterns, bro. I've stared at it from every angle for a century. But what do you see?"

"I see that I was wrong," I say, lost in the grotesque display.

"Wrong about what?" Mary says returning with a platter of food that could feed ten armies or maybe one Manny.

"When I stumbled onto this place I thought I'd found an office or a headquarters or something. But that's not it at all."

"What is it then?"

"It's a church."

Chapter 21

Manny and Mary's jaws drop as they look around the recreation of the hundred-year-old room. They've looked at it a thousand times before, but they're seeing it with brand new eyes.

"This mark here," Manny says moving to one end of the room. "Like ash was ground into and these deep indentations next to it. Holy crap, man. There was an altar here."

I nod. "Burnt offerings, probably. Probably some of the victims whose bodies were never found. Or animal sacrifices. Or both."

Mary moves a little deeper into the room with eyes wide and deep as vinyl records. She holds her arms wide just a few feet from the far wall. "This would have been where the cult image was. A statue of the thing they worshiped which, I'd be willing to bet, was some kind of snake."

"I would not take that bet," I say.

"Why would they put their weirdo church in the basement of a luxury resort, though?" Manny asks.

"It makes sense to me," I offer. "Anybody from anywhere in the world, including powerful people, could come here and even stay for extended periods of time without it being weird or suspect. Great rooms, great service, great food at a dozen five-star restaurants. And it's huge. Once you're inside, if you're one of them, you could disappear down to the basement and it wouldn't be at all weird that nobody could find you. You might be getting a massage or at the pool or in the sauna. It's a pretty perfect cover, really. I assume somebody looked into who owns the place after I got put on ice?"

"Of course," says Mary. "It was owned by a shell corporation in France that was owned by a shell corporation in Japan that was owned by a shell corporation in China which, as far as anyone could tell, and a lot of really smart people tried really hard to tell, had no employees and whose only other holding was a used mattress store that went out of business in 1974."

"People sell used mattresses?" I ask, fighting back the bile rising up in my throat.

"Yeah. It's super gross. Thus the out-of-business part, I'd imagine. Anyway, nobody alive or dead could be connected to the ownership of the resort."

"Taxes," I say. "They had to pay taxes and that's the sort of thing where records never die."

Mary shakes her head. "They tried that, too. Taxes were paid by an accounting firm that never laid eyes on their client. They received documents by email from an untraceable sender and the firm was paid from a numbered account in the Cayman Islands. Every road leads to a brick wall dead end."

"Somebody built the dang thing!" I say getting a little testier than I meant to.

"We know who built it, but that goes nowhere, too. It was an unrelated company. They sold it to the ghost corp about ten years before you shot their employees of the month through the gut. Sold it for about six times the value of the place, too."

"And they were paid from an untraceable numbered account."

"You got it. Every single employee, independent contractor, and frequent guest was interviewed and cleared. Even the general manager who ran the whole operation had only been there six months and knew nothing. He was hired by the guy he was replacing who was hired by the guy he was replacing who was—" "I get it. There was essentially no boss. Ever. And everyone was paid enough money to not ask too many questions." I swear a little. "These people are good."

Many smiles. "If they weren't friggin' amazing this would have been solved and stopped literally thousands of years ago. And you wouldn't be our only hope."

I go back to studying the room. Something here wants to talk to me. I just need to know how to listen.

"I can't believe they didn't have a plan to destroy this evidence," I say as I continue to take in as much detail as I can. "They were so careful, so batcrap-crazy careful in every other aspect, and they didn't have a backup plan in case some nosey detective was able to track them down here?"

"They did have a plan. This was a burn room. It was a burn resort, really. They rigged the whole place with thermite. Enough bad stuff making fires hot enough to turn not just everything in here to ash, but the entire hotel above too. That stuff reaches temps higher than the surface of the sun, kyah. No joke. Even the metal in those swords would have just been puddles if they triggered it."

I nod my head. It makes sense that they'd have an almost literal scorched earth policy. "So why didn't they burn it?" I ask.

"You'll like this, bro. When you went through the wall like the dang Kool-Aid man, you just happened to take out the main electric cable connected to the remote trigger. Ripped the sucker right out of the receiver and broke their ability to set the thing off. You bricked their burn room, man! You're one lucky son of a gun." "Lucky is definitely how I felt that day. And every day really."

Manny looks a little serious again, which is always disconcerting. "Between the guests and workers, you saved about 600 lives that day. Saved them from boiling to death and dying screaming. Hard to come up with a much better way to go out than to do it keeping your brothers and sisters safe."

I don't say it, but that really does mean a lot to me. And I can tell Manny knows that. I don't know if my life ever meant much of anything, but just maybe my death did and I'll take it.

I turn back to the blades on the wall and gaze at them like they might share a secret or two if I just stare them down long enough. "I want to hold one. I feel like maybe it wants to tell me something."

"Is that something you'd like?" Manny says with a smile. He snaps his fingers and says, "Abracadabra" because he is, above all else, a nerd, and a pedestal rises from the floor with one of the blades on it. The whole spectacle is a little showy for my taste, but I asked and he made it happen so I don't much feel like complaining. "It's real?" I ask. "Not a hologram or a replica?"

"Hundred percent. The genuine article. I had a thief trained from birth for maximum sneak nick it from a police storage warehouse a couple of years ago to study it."

"Mary smiles. He loves to brag on me."

"I do!"

We've still got dogs and fathers still love their daughters. Maybe we'll survive the future after all. "I tried to get one as soon as I knew they existed, but it took me forty years to track one down. Some powerful people didn't want anyone knowing much about them." I reach toward the sword but then pull back a bit. "May I?"

"Yeah, brother. But be careful. The venom is still on there and may still be potent. I don't know. I'm not a snake juice doctor. But back in the day fully 3 CSUs died from accidental cuts just taking them off the wall. Just one little nick and done. Dead. Last rites and whatnot, kyah."

I nod and take the evil instrument in hand. I turn it over and over. It's just a thing. Just metal, wood and leather. A fine thing, though. No doubt. The material is beyond top shelf by several degrees, and the craftsmanship is ludicrous. If I didn't know it killed someone who didn't deserve it I'd call this blade "beautiful." "Did you learn anything from it?" I ask.

"I think so. But I want to see what you see first."

"I assume you sourced everything."

"The steel is Chinese. From Anshan in Liaoning to be precise."

I read a book about China once and I remember a thing or two. "The most common spot in the country to make steel, right?"

"Bingo is your name O."

"Is it stamped?" I felt dumb asking that but also felt like I had to.

"Forged. By someone who really knew what they were doing. I've shown it to at least a thousand blacksmiths, swordsmiths, and silversmiths around the world and the work doesn't remind them of anyone. But they all agree it's redonk."

I have to laugh at that. I wonder how many multibillionaires in history have ever used the word "redonk."

"So the metal is common. The wood on the handle on the other hand…that looks unusual. I'm gonna guess teak."

"Quebracho."

That word does something funny in my head. It bounces around like it has a home somewhere in there but it can't find it. "Why is that word familiar?" "Maybe just from trivia or something?" Manny guesses. "It's the hardest wood in the world. Twice as strong as Osage Orange. The name means 'ax breaker' in Spanish."

"Well that's a pretty badass name for a tree."

"Comes from the Gran Chaco region of South America."

"Which is where?"

"Bolivia, Argentina, Paraguay"

I nod as if that means anything to me and make a mental note to find a map. "I swear I've heard that word before. I just can't place it. Say it again, please."

"Quebracho."

It bangs around again, but it doesn't make itself known to me. So I move on. "The leather the handle is wrapped in? It feels plush. Ultra-luxurious even after a century of sitting around."

"It's crocodile. Usually used for super high-end handbags and boots and whatnot."

An image of something or rather someone is starting to form in my mind. I fight off the smile that wants to curl the corners of my mouth, though, because it's too wild and unsubstantiated.

"That was my best shot at finding these guys, I think," Manny says. "I traced it to a specific species, the Nile crocodile. There are only a handful of people who farm them in the whole world. But by the time I got my hands on one, every single known owner and operator of a Nile Crocodile farm that could have produced these wraps was dead. In fact, they were all dead before you found the place."

"Covering their tracks before they made any tracks. It's psychotic and probably how they've never been caught. You do know the old riddle, what's the only way two people keep a secret?"

Manny smiles, "If one of them is dead."

I turn the sword over in my hand. There are markings on the handle, beneath the wrap, that I can just make out the edges of. "These carvings on the handle," I say. "Snakes I'm guessing."

"Yeah. But not particularly like any snake art that's come before. Nothing to lead to an artist. I checked with every illustrator, painter, art history teacher, and museum curator in the universe. Twice. I've been at this for a century, remember."

I nod to let him know I understand, but my eyes don't leave the blade. "The serpents are carved into the ax breaker wood. You can't just do that with a knife, right? To even machine it you'd need something crazy hard."

"Tungsten carbide," Manny says. "Tungsten carbide with a coating of polycrystalline diamond, as a matter of fact. That's what you need to carve the ax breaker." "Were those rare as hen's teeth back then by any chance?"

"Not really. I went down that path, too. You could get a five-piece set of 'em for about 400 bucks at just about any decent hardware store."

"Okay," I say. "So you add it all up. Who or what in 2025 was ordering large amounts of Chinese steel, ax breaker wood, crocodile leather, tungsten carbide drill bits with diamond coating, and inland taipan snake venom. Surely there aren't many places where all of those things intersected. I mean, surely if we could find anyone buying all of that they can at least lead us somewhere."

Manny smiles a sad smile. "Not if it was all purchased on black markets and on the dark web, kyah. And not if all those people ended up dead before anyone knew to ask them anything. I tried that myself and I found that nobody on the whole stupid planet could be shown buying all of that stuff. And anyone buying one or even a couple of them seemed to have good enough reason for it. Like they made super expensive handbags."

My detective tingle is telling me it's about the tree. "Say the name of the wood again, please. The ax breaker."

"Quebracho, bro. Dang, being dead for a few decades did some bad Joo Joo to your brain hole. You want me to write it down for you?"

"Yes," I say. "That's exactly what I want."

Manny moves his hand through the air like he's painting or something, and electric blue lines follow from the tip of his finger and linger in the space between us. He's writing with light right there in front of me. And when he's done, "Quebracho" is spelled out before my eyes. And I see it. I recognize the word as soon as I see it. I know where I've read that before.

And I'm pretty sure I know who killed me. And a whole lot of other people.

Chapter 22

Mary and Manny look at me like I'm an idiot. Which, to be fair, is accurate. But I think I'm onto something here.

Then at once, in stereo, they both burst out laughing which does feel a little rude and, I'm not going to lie, hurts my feelings a little bit.

"You think Buster Guff is behind the cult?" they both ask, still in stereo. Then there's more laughing. They actually double over and grab their tummies. They move the same and laugh with the same cadence. She's a mini Manny and it's weird that I find her so attractive.

"Why is this funny?"

"Well, bro," Manny says in between guffaws. "For one thing, Buster Guff is an idiot. A tier one, top shelf, premium, AAA-certified moron. Dumb as a bag of hammers. There is simply no way he could run an international murder syndicate that never gets caught. I doubt that dude could run a microwave oven, bro. And for a second thing, he's been dead almost as long as you have."

That one takes me a second to process. I have to admit it's a pretty good alibi. "But I saw him last night. On a…I don't know, billboard or whatever. A screen that took up the side of a building. He was shilling for the company that tried to kill me as soon as I stopped being dead."

"Yes," Mary says, her giggle-fit coming to an end I hope. "A lot of the companies he used to own still trot out facsimiles of him in hologram or CGI or whatever.

"It's really no different from how Americans still use George Washington to sell each other dining tables and bedsheets or whatever. He's a mascot. He was only ever a mascot. He tricked the whole world into thinking he was brilliant because he was the richest man in history at the time, and people are hard-wired to think riches and genius are the same. But his empire was all built on inherited fortune and really shady deals to take over other people's companies and then retroactively take credit for them. He hired armies, literal armies of kids to stalk social media and brag on him and it worked. For a small time, anyway. But he was just a spoiled rich kid who never had a thought he didn't steal from someone better. He was just another emperor with no clothes. And then it ended as dumb as it possibly could have, I guess. Which was very on brand. He died trying to make a solid gold cast of his own genitals."

"What? Why?" I say trying and failing to fight off the typhoon of imagery that sentence cannonballed right into my brain.

Mary again looks at me like I was born yesterday on a turnip truck. "So he could spend…um…quality time with himself. But in gold." "Thank you for that. I hate it."

"But he didn't make, like, a plaster cast first. Because he was an idiot. Or maybe he just so got so high he started to believe the things he paid kids to say about him and he believed he was some kind of superhuman or something. I don't know. But he just dipped his bits right into a crucible of molten gold, man. Burned 'em right off."

Manny and I both recoil from that. Surely Manny already knew the story, but that's not the kind of thing you can ever get used to thinking about I don't think.

"And burned a hole in his femoral artery, too," She continues. "It was a really big deal at the time. Took a few months before we all stopped laughing."

With this new information, my mind knows it needs to pivot, but it won't. "It all makes too much sense to be nothing," I say. "I swear I can't be this wrong. So maybe he was an idiot. I don't have any trouble at all believing that. Maybe whoever was really in charge of his car company ran the cult. I don't know. And they didn't run it. Maybe they were just in charge of acquisitions or murder knife production. But they are involved. I know it."

"What makes you so sure, detective?"

"When I went through the wall in that room…this room but for real…when I killed those serpents and ran through the wall, I fell into the parking garage and onto one of his cars—A 2025 Vinci." I hold up the blade for emphasis. "And the leather felt and looked and smelled exactly like this."

"You remember that after all this time?" Mary asks with more than a little doubt in her voice.

"It was two days ago. For me it was barely forty-eight hours since I smelled it. And it's distinctive. Yes. I'm sure. The seats were Nile Crocodile leather. Why wouldn't they be? Buster was all about conspicuous, nonsense wealth, right? He lived in a giant cube made of titanium, didn't he? He had a servant who did nothing but hold an umbrella over his head even when he was indoors. Of course he'd have insane upholstery in his cars. And a car company could buy all the crocodile leather and Chinese steel and diamond drill bits they like and nobody would think twice."

"Because they have good reason to, bro." Manny says sceptically.

"But the thing that makes me so sure is, when I looked at the dash it was wooden. A dark, rich wod that I'd never seen before. And carved into it was a word I couldn't pronounce at the time, but now that I've seen it again I'm certain. The word was 'quebracho.' He couldn't help himself. He had to brag out loud about having the hardest, rarest, most expensive wood in the world in that car."

Manny raises an eyebrow and Mary follows suit. It's crazy how much they look alike despite Mary also looking like an angel and Manny looking like a thing bears run screaming from. "Hang on," he says, swiping his hands through the air like he's navigating something I can't see. "The internet isn't what it used to be since A-S-P bought it but—"

"Buster's company bought the entire internet?" Mary nods almost like she's guilty for letting it happen. Like it was her fault somehow.

Manny goes on, "But surely…huh. That's weird. Super weird."

"What?" I ask more impatiently than I intended.

"There are no specs of the Vinci's from 2025 anywhere. No photos. No blurbs or articles about it. No nothing. Like it's a ghost car. Huh. Looks like they…yeah, they were all recalled that year for unspecified reasons. And every owner was given a 2026 model as reimbursement."

"That's weird, right?" I ask.

"It's weird that they scrubbed all the photos, but they may have just been embarrassed it was such a lemon. The recall is massive, and the timing is suspect as heck, but like half of all Vincis were recalled every year. They had a tendency to spontaneously combust, bro. Because Buster was crap at everything I'm telling you. So I think your logic is pretty tight. I respect that agile brain hole, kyah. But there's no way to test your theory. Those cars have been gone for a century. Kinda like you."

I smile a smile that only ever means "let's get dangerous." I'm about to have a really bad idea and I love it.

"Not all of them are gone," I say. "You guys said it yourselves. The one I died in is in the crime museum right here in downtown Dubai."

"That museum is guarded almost as tight as the moon," Mary says. "We can't just walk in and take samples. So how does that help us?"

I smile that smile again. "It's time for a good old-fashioned heist." Then I take a beat for dramatic effect and say, "Let's go rob a museum."

Mary's eyes light up like a child at a candy store. Manny's eyes narrow like a father who's worried about his daughter.

They ask for a few minutes together and huddle at the end of the room. I make an elaborate show of looking at the sword to help sell the lie that I'm not listening.

But I'm doing everything I can to eavesdrop.

It's hard to make out too much, but I think I hear things like, "It's the best shot we've had in years," and "It's too dangerous," and "This is exactly why we woke him up," and "*We* didn't do nothing! You woke him up."

Mary seems to be reminding Manny that she trained from birth to be an outlaw. Manny seems to be reminding Mary that these people already killed him and he won't see her lost, too.

"What's the point in being alive like this?" I think she asks. "This isn't living. This is just being afraid in the dark."

They lower their voices further and further until it's all lost to me. But soon enough they come back to my end of the room and Manny says something I definitely did not see coming.

"All right, kyah. We'll do it. But first I have to put a bomb in your head."

Chapter 23

Before I know what's really happening I'm strapped down to a metal table, my nose pressed against cold, brushed steel, and wondering not for the first time in my life if these people are really my friends.

"Why in the name of all that is holy would you need to put a bomb in my head?" I ask as if there were an answer to that question that would make this not insane.

Mary produces a syringe from somewhere that looks like a small, but not that small, handgun. The gauge of it is ludicrous. A good-sized mouse could pass through the hole in this needle. She puts on some rubber gloves either to protect against germs or to complete her supervillain look.

"I assume you've noticed that everyone you meet here has a glow from the base of their skull?" Mary asks. "The orange lights. Yes. I did think those were pretty weird. Wait. Those are bombs?"

Manny leans down so I can better see him with my face smooshed against the table. "Those are your identity here. It's your driver's license, your credit card, your keys, your vaccination history, your dang college transcripts. Everything that documents you as you and everything that allows you to operate in this world is contained inside a little goober about the size of an ibuprofen pill."

"Goober, I assume is a technical term."

"Highly technical. Yes. Don't mock the dead billionaire tech industry tycoon while he's about to inject you with explodey machines."

It's a fair point, I admit to myself, but my only response is to offer the best shrug I can manage given the leather straps forcing me to hug a table so tightly I can hear my own pulse.

"The goober is also a GPS tag. A thing that allows you to be tracked anywhere you go. And it can, if necessary, render you unable to cause trouble. Or to speak. Or to retain mastery over your own bladder."

"If you step out of line somebody blows up your head!" I shout as I try to wiggle free of the restraints. They are really not selling me on this.

Manny laughs a little more nervously than usual. "It's just a small electric pulse. In theory. Like an EMP for your central nervous system. It just shuts you down temporarily. But they have been known to malfunction and…boom."

And suddenly, Moza telling me there's no more crime makes a lot of sense. Every person in this hellscape future essentially has a loaded gun, a global positioning satellite, and a camera pointed at them at all times.

I say, "Okay, there is no way in any world, future or not, that I'm letting you put a dang stick of dynamite in my head, Manny!"

"Relax, kyah. And stop wriggling or she might screw this up and paralyze you or decapitate you or something. We're not putting a real bomb in you. This one is basically a skeleton key without the EMP. I can upload any identity I want into it so you can go about the city without anyone knowing who you are or what you're up to. It'll fool all the sensors and security things and whatnot. You couldn't get within a kilometre of the museum without it. At least not without being detected and detained. But this one can't be activated to shut you down or blow you up. Not by them and not by anyone. It reads like a normal IDB but it's inert. You can trust me."

Mary steps toward me with the needle. "This is why the drones came after us in the desert. They detected a life sign with no IDB. That's short for, 'identity beacon.' They're out there to stop unwanted travellers from accessing Dubai. Invaders. Spies. Rogue armies. What have you. They don't even want you within several kilos of the place. So the drones detain you before you get too close to the city. At least they do if you aren't real handy with duct tape and storms. Even if you can avoid or outrun the murder bots, though, you can't get into the city without an IDB saying you're a citizen. Unless you're in a car my dad built that can spoof the doors. Since he built the dome, he can find ways around it."

"I leave a hundred backdoors in all my code, bro. It's just good safety sense. And also I can still rob just about anybody I want, which is useful."

"Once we got you inside, the drones assumed you belong here so they stopped trying to murder us to death, but you can't get through any security checkpoints inside the city without one of these. And there's gonna be dozens of checkpoints between us and that car you died in. So we gotta give you a fake IDB if you want to get anywhere with this investigation. It won't hurt. I'll see to that."

"I can't believe you let people do this to you! This is bonkers. People here are barely people, man. Why don't they fight back?"

"There's no conviction in this world, detective," Mary says sadly. "No passion. No fight. That's why I had to wake you up. That's why you're our only hope. There's no one left here with the will to win. There's barely anyone with the will to live. We're just…here." Manny takes over, "When it started, when the IDBs were first introduced, it seemed like an ultimate convenience. A cool body mod that meant you'd never lose your keys or your wallet again. Some people were worried about being tracked and whatnot, of course, but while you were alive everyone agreed to carry a smartphone which was, at the time, the most sophisticated surveillance tech in the world. It's just human nature to sacrifice privacy for comfort. And pretty quickly, just like with smartphones, it became nearly impossible to make it through daily life without one. Couldn't enrol in schools or get a job if you weren't chipped. Couldn't get a table at a restaurant or operate a television. And a decade or so in, when they were impossible to get by without, that's when they added the EMP. They do it at birth, now. Right there in the hospital. And if you try to remove it…boom. No more head, kyah."

"I'm going to take a wild, shot in the dark, detective's intuition stab at this and say that the company in charge of all this is A-S-P."

Manny smiles a guilty smile, "Got it in one." "For the love of monkeys, Manny! You guys may have given the power of life and death over everyone in the city to the serpent cult! And even if you didn't, you gave it to a corporation which is almost as bad!"

"I didn't do it, man! I fought back so hard they killed me, remember? I may have lost but I did go down fighting.

"Just like you, kyah. And just like everyone else who stood up to them, I guess. Which is why nobody stands up to them. But I didn't let them get Mary. She was born free range right here in my fortress. Her chip is just like yours. Inert and able to read as anyone we want her to be."

"And we're still fighting," says Mary. "One of us kept going after death. So don't look down your 21st century nose at the two of us. I mean to stop this horror show finally. You're my latest and best weapon. But, yeah, we really screwed this pooch pretty good as a society. That's why we have to fix it!"

"And at no point did you stop to wonder if they were evil snake killers while they put explosives in everyone's heads?"

"I knew they were evil, bro. But the idea that they were also the cult is just…if you're right about them we are so totally screwed, man."

I sigh and relax as best I can while tied to a metal table. "Just do it," I say.

First Mary gives me something to numb my neck and head. And it works, thank goodness. I hear a *whoosh* sound and I feel a bit of pressure and I know there's something inside of me that shouldn't be there.

I know more than ever that I'm going to kill whoever did this to the world. But I don't know if that'll be enough. I just don't know if we can win.

Mary unstraps me and I stand up and rub the back of my neck. There's a bump but there's no pain.

Oh, but the pain is coming, I silently promise the world.

The pain is coming.

Chapter 24

The idea of preserving and immortalizing horrors feels weird, but crime museums aren't uncommon. Something in human nature wants to stare into the darkness living somewhere inside us all. It's why crime movies and books and things are also always everywhere.

At the museum called Alcatraz East, in the US, you can see the 1968 Volkswagen Beetle that once belonged to arguably the world's most famous murderer Ted Bundy. And right next to that you can check out the 1993 white Ford Bronco O.J. Simpson used to take the LAPD on history's dumbest car chase.

Jack the Ripper, the world's first known serial who terrorized Whitechapel in 1888 has a museum all to himself in London. In Las Vegas, there's the Mob Museum which looks to expand our understanding of organized crime throughout the years. And, since it's Vegas, for the truly deranged couple they do offer a wedding package. Get married and have your reception surrounded by Al Capone's bedroom set or whatever.

And if you're feeling particularly gruesome, head over to Rothberg, Germany for the Medieval Crime and Justice Museum, where you can explore medieval and early modern torture devices, shame punishments, and various doodads used to carry out corporal punishment back when things like forcing folk to sit in a chair made of iron spikes seemed like a fine way to spend an afternoon.

The thing that's bananas about the Museum of Modern Crime in this 22nd century Dubai, at least to my scrambled brain, is it's almost all about crimes that haven't happened yet. Well, they haven't happened for me. Everyone else's history is my future. Or it was, I guess.

As with most things in life, there's no going back.

Here you can learn about a lady called The Squirrel Mother. She operated in Italy in the 2040s and trained a small army of attack rodents to carry out various crimes. Mostly she killed people she had grudges against, two ex-husbands, the barista who spelled her name wrong every morning, a critic who hated her favorite television show. Though she dabbled in theft as well. Apparently you'd be amazed what a well-organized battalion of squirrels can lift when they work together.

She was, unbelievably, finally caught when police trained their own squirrel to infiltrate her militia. The small, furry officer led officers right to the Mother's hideout which, perfectly, was a treehouse deep in the Foreste Casentinesi.

Honestly, I can't believe I slept through Operation Undercover Squirrel.

Sadly, all of the animals were euthanized following her arrest. Several of them were stuffed and can be viewed here at the museum, posed in various menacing ways as their corpses re-enact some of the crimes they were forced to commit.

Another popular exhibit details a crime syndicate that sold bootleg bottles of Evian and Perrier all across the globe during the Water Wars. They made their money keeping the ultra-rich hydrated but used the cash to keep the agua flowing to some of the most impoverished communities around the globe. It's estimated that over the span of twelve years they saved six hundred million lives. They were all found and executed in Russia for the sin of helping the poor to resources the wealthy wanted.

Maybe my favorite display teaches us about Trevor Barkley, an eleven-year-old child who found his way into some of the source code for *Meta Earth*, the world's most popular virtual reality universe in the 2050s. He hacked the code until he had given his own avatar superpowers and used them to deface and destroy every virtual billboard and advertisement in the system. He created an entire world without marketing. Without sales. He destroyed trillions of dollars' worth of real-world value to create a place where people could escape being told what they need to buy and be and look like in order to be happy. And he did it wearing a rainbow cape because he was a boss. The end result was that people were the happiest they've ever been.

For a time, people lived entire virtual lives without being told they weren't good enough and how much to spend until they were. It was the closest to free any of them ever felt, they all said. And they loved Trevor for it. They built statues of him in the *Meta Earth*. Wrote songs about him. He never asked for a thing.

Hundreds of thousands of agents were deputized to kill Trevor's avatar. To stop him so they could start selling stuff again. But Trevor made himself a superman. He was invulnerable. Unkillable. They went to war with this child in this virtual space with digital tanks and guns and eventually with other superpowered people they created and he beat them all back. So the powers that be did the only thing they could think of, they killed every single other person in the world. They nuked every continent, every city, every town, and every living creature. Burned them to ash. Full scorched Earth. Only Trevor could survive the onslaught. He was left alone on the charred remains of a dead planet he tried to save.

It broke Trevor. He started seeing a therapist. She turned him in to the authorities for a virtual penthouse apartment in the new fake world they launched.

He was tried and convicted of about a hundred things. He's still in prison in Brazil.

If I survive this insane mission that I definitely will not survive, I plan to break Trevor out of jail.

I could stay here learning about the crimes of future past for weeks, honestly. But of course, none of that is why we are here today.

In the back room of the third floor, where very few people seem to care about it, next to a plaque with my face on it that lists my year of death as 2025, is the 2025 Vinci Model Q that I stole and drove for a half kilometre or so before they got me. Just looking at it all smashed up and mangled, seeing way too many litres of my own dried blood on the seats and the dash, sends me momentarily back to that place and that time. For just a second, I feel it all again. The panic, the impact, the pain. The fact that my final thought was about her.

I guess I don't hide the flashback that shot through me because Mary squeezes my arm lightly and asks if I'm okay. "Yeah," I say. "It's just…"

"It was only about 48 hours ago for you," she finishes my thought for me. "Look. We've waited a hundred years to get you back on this case. We can wait a few more days if you need to get your head right."

"No," I say. "I'm good." I want to see this through. I want an end to it all.

Manny was as good as always. His skeleton key IDBs allowed us to sail through the various security checkpoints on the way here. I'm a retired architect named Kareem, apparently. Mary is a personal shopper named Zara. Nobody looked twice at us.

There is no reason to think we aren't who we say we are. We are both dressed to the nines and looking sharp as a couple of tacks if I do say so myself. I am in a perfectly tailored tan suit that came out of one of those magic cabinets to my exact fit. Mary is wearing a red dress of some kind that hugs her in ways that are making everyone here jealous. Her ensemble is completed by a ludicrously huge ruby ring that may be fake or may be worth more than the building we're standing in. Neither would surprise me.

There are cameras all over the place, covering every conceivable angle of this place. I guess nothing makes you paranoid quite like cataloguing eons of murder and mayhem.

There are also several security guards around, but they're just as slight, pale, and sickly as everyone else I see around here. A whole world of men and women whisper-thin. As fine as a bee's wings. A good breeze might blow them away.

I've lived my life on the right side of the law, more or less. I've bent a few trespassing regulations here and there and maybe there's been some light wire fraud in service of my clients as a P.I., but for the most part, I really do try to keep my nose clean. But, like most people I assume, I have always wanted to pull off a spectacular heist. Something straight out of *Oceans 11* or *The Italian Job*. Something clever and crafty and bold. Manny, though, has made this job a little too easy. He's taken most of the challenge out, the enormous genius that he is.

I told him we'd need a crybaby, something to distract people while we grab what we need. He led us into another large room in his dungeon and opened up his workbench, a wild, electric thing that looked like a motorcycle from *Tron* had a baby with an apothecary table from Ikea, and had just the thing we needed synthesized in no time.

I told him we'd need the cameras to all die for a few seconds. Same trick. Same ludicrous speed. He made up a goober like he was griddling up pancakes. Easy as Sunday morning breakfast.

And, yes, I have fully leaned into the technical term "goober."

"Lastly," I said to him, "We're gonna need basically a small lightsabre."

Manny laughed and shut down his workbench. He just opened a nearby cabinet revealing dozens of ornate cylinders of various sizes and colors with different intricate designs and things.

"Just pick one, bro," he said. "I've been making lightsabres since I was three! Lost a couple of toes that way but it was worth it!"

And that was that. We made our way here.

The Crime Museum is, like most large buildings in this century and the last, made almost entirely of glass and steel. Unlike most buildings, this one is shaped like a magnifying glass. One assumes to evoke Sherlock

Holmes, the greatest crime-fighter who never lived. It was built not long after I died and has been renovated and updated several times throughout the years.

One of the dream scenarios for the heist would be to hotwire the Vinci, drive it right out the dang window, and down the road like I'm in a *Fast and Furious* movie or something.

I can see it all in my mind. The glass shattering, the car flying through the air as it falls the two stories to the street, wind in our hair, both of us feeling all kinds of Vin Diesel. Maybe a rock ballad plays as we descend in slow motion. It's a nice image and I want to do it.

The problems with that plan, of course, are legion. The car hasn't moved on its own in a hundred years. It was totalled when I was mostly killed. It certainly doesn't have any juice left in the battery. The engine was probably destroyed by the truck that hit me. And even if it weren't, it certainly would be by falling two stories to the ground. So sadly, that particular fantasy is not to be.

Luckily, we don't need the car. We just need a few small bits from it.

The crybaby Manny built for us is actually a dozen cry-babies. They're about the size of a postage stamp. As Mary and I perused the exhibits we each placed a stamp on a window around the gallery. Each one contains a supersonic emitter. A speaker the size of an ant that can blast sounds like it's a Marshall stack turned to eleven.

Basically, when Mary pushes a button hidden in her ring, each stamp is going to scream. Manny took the term 'crybaby' a bit literally.

But even all that is too subtle for Manny. Each stamp is going to scream at a frequency that should shatter anything made of glass within fifteen meters. We're going to blow the windows off the joint. Literally. At the same time, Mary's ring will also take out all of the cameras for four seconds. Then we use the cigarette-sized lightsabres Manny gave us to carve a few samples from the car like we're serving roast duck.

What could go wrong?

Mary gives me a look like she's still unsure if I'm steady enough for this. I try to look like I am and my guess is I'm around forty percent successful.

She looks a good deal more serious than I've seen her. She takes thievery pretty seriously. I like that in a burglar. Anything worth doing is worth doing right. "You good, detective?" She asks.

"Five by five."

She gives me a nod. "In three." I return the nod.

I count down in my head.

Mary flips open the gajillion carat ruby on her ring revealing a small red button.

She pushes it.

The sound of the screams is deafening. Like a baby goat the size of a jet landing inside your head.

And moments later the whole world seems to explode into a hail of glass shards.

Everybody shouts and everybody runs and everybody ducks for cover.

Everybody except me and Mary, that is. We leap into action. We practiced it a hundred times in Manny's weird simulation room so we'd leave little to chance and the likelihood of one of us losing a few toes on the blades is minimal.

We ignite the lightsabers which aren't made of light or lasers. They're essentially tiny plasma torches, but they look the part and they work like a treat. Mine is blue and Mary's is red and I figure I'll deal with the potential implications of that later.

We step over the velvet rope surrounding the Vinci and an alarm sounds and nobody cares because the building is exploding.

We need three samples. Leather. Steel. Wood. I'm on the leather. I've got a small circle, about the size of a gold doubloon, off the headrest and into my pocket before the glass hits the floor.

Mary hits the deck and does a little ninja roll around the back of the car. She's got a ringlet worth of tailpipe off and she's on her feet in an instant.

Then, staying low, she leans through the shattered passenger side window and cuts a small chunk of ax breaker from the dash.

We're a well-practiced, well-oiled machine. The whole operation takes two seconds. Tops. We planned everything we would do and executed it flawlessly.

What we did not plan for, was the X-factor.

Everyone should have run and hid from the sound and the glass and everyone did. All but one person.

When I step back from the ropes I notice the one individual who didn't duck and cover. And I'd guess she noticed the alarms we tripped.

Moza is staring right at me and her gun is drawn.

Chapter 25

For a few seconds, maybe longer, maybe a day or a week, I don't know, I just stand there staring at her. Part of me is in shock and part of me maybe thinks that in the future women are like T-Rexes and their vision is based on movement.

Maybe I'm just an idiot.

Mary snaps me out of it by saying, "So we run now, right? Running seems good."

I nod but my body won't move. I'm frozen not by fear but by, I think, my desire not to let this woman down. Or, really, the late grandmother that she looks almost exactly like.

"We use our feet for that," Mary says with a growl of frustration. "Feet and legs. Let's go."

I resolve to do it, but I don't have a chance to twitch a single muscle before Moza yells, "Freeze! Hands in the air!"

"Moza," I say, raising my arms as I was told, "I promise I'm doing something that needs done. Something important. Your grandmother would approve."

"I wish I could believe that," she says, the hint of a tear dotting the corner of her left eye. "Turn around and get on your knees."

Mary leans into me, her lips nanometres from my ear, and says, "Don't breathe."

She then takes the ruby off of her ring and slams it onto the floor. It explodes into an enormous puff of smoke like someone just doused a campfire. The thick grey haze fills the room. I try to hold my breath but I'm only mostly successful.

I hear Moza coughing and gagging as Mary grabs my arm and pulls me away. I want to help her more than I want to escape, but more than that I want to save the world.

But more than that I want to hurt the people who took everything from me. So I run.

"Why am I crying?" I ask Mary as we bolt down the emergency exit stairs.

"Capsasian in the smoke bomb!" she yells back as she bursts through the door to the lower level. Most people are still ducking and covering. The fractal patterns of the shattered glass on the floor make me smile for a moment for reasons I don't really understand. There's beauty in them.

"Basically," she says, "It's like rubbing your eyes after cutting jalapenos. Everyone will be just fine."

We make a break for the entrance when we see Moza coming down the main staircase cutting us off. She's still coughing but not slowing down. "I said freeze!" she wheezes more than yells across the room.

We stop, make a hard right turn, and head for one of the broken windows that leads to a side street.

"You think they'll make an exhibit at the crime museum about the time someone robbed the crime museum?" Mary asks as we leap through the shattered window frame. "I bet I look good on a plaque!"

I ignore her and look back. Moza is hot on our heels. She's faster than me by a lot. Modern nutrition or training or just great genes or all three, I don't know, but I'm not outrunning her on foot. And suddenly I wonder if everyone here is really as frail as they look. Maybe they're secretly hard as nails.

I take the leather headrest sample from my pocket and press it into Mary's hand. "Get clear. I'll draw her away." Mary looks at me uneasily. "I'm sure," I say. She takes the leather with a nod.

Outside on the street she turns left and I turn right. From the corner of my vision, I see Mary climb the side of a building like she's gosh darn Spider-Man. And in a blink, she's gone. Good.

Moza follows me just as I figured she would. I'm the one who hurt her. People don't really ever change. Not in the ways that make us human and soft and vulnerable.

I cut down a dark alley and I think of all the times I was on the other end of a chase like this. My biggest advantage in those races was always that I knew the city better than the guy I was running down. It's just not true anymore. I don't recognize this world. I can't navigate it. And I get punished for it as the alley dead ends. I'm surrounded by high walls on three sides with a very angry lady with a gun on the fourth. I stop and raise my hands above my head.

"Turn around slowly," Moza says.

I do as I'm asked. Her shiny silver pistol is pointed right at my chest.

"Get on your knees!" she demands.

I shake my head. "I'm not gonna do that, Moza. Just listen to me. Please."

"I'm an officer of the law! And I don't even know you." She pulls the trigger.

Chapter 26

Moza looks pretty confused when nothing happens after she pulls the trigger. So she pulls it again. And again. She gives it a look and shakes it in her hand like it's a TV remote with a dead battery. It's adorable.

"That's not going to work," I say. "Your gun connects to an IDB to shut down a body's nervous system. But the chip in my skull doesn't have the kill switch."

"Fine," she declares as she marches toward me. "I'll do it manually." She grabs one of my wrists and tries to bend it behind my back to cuff me. She's fast but she's not strong and I don't move.

"I'm sorry. I can't let that happen. What I'm doing is too important."

"Robbing a museum is too important to get arrested?" She says putting both arms and all her weight into twisting my wrist. I still don't budge. It's like wrestling a toddler. "Can we get some coffee, please? And I'll fill you in. Then if you still want to arrest me I won't resist."

She tries a few more times to wrangle my arms into cuffs but it's just never going to happen and soon enough she admits defeat with a sigh. "One cup. And then you come quietly if I don't like what you have to say. Deal."

We find a quiet little coffee shop not far from what's left of the museum and I ask the server, who I'm about eighty percent sure is a robot, for the largest cup of black coffee they offer. The only three patrons in the shop when we arrive leave immediately and I start to wonder if I smell. Moza reads it on my face.

"You're a big guy, Khalifa. You're a foot taller than everyone you'll meet and you can see your muscles through your suit. You don't belong here. You don't look like humans look anymore. And the people of this world are trained from birth to fear things that don't belong. From what I've read, it wasn't that different when you come from."

The coffee arrives and I'm pleasantly surprised to find it's roughly the size of a garbage can. I take a single sip and almost involuntarily I sigh with pleasure.

"Flavor country," I say. "Whatever coffee magic you guys work in the future is almost worth missing the last century." "So," she says with an impatient wave of her hand,

"spill it."

I squint at her to get a read, to see if she's on my side or not. I can't tell what's going on behind those gorgeous eyes, but that's nothing new for the women in her family. "Why were you there tonight? Were you following me?"

"No. After you came to see me I just started thinking about…all of it. You and the cult that killed my grandmother and I wanted to remember. I wanted to refresh my knowledge on what the heck actually happened. I thought that would be a good place to do it. I didn't know I was going to witness the crime of the decade."

"Oh come on! All I did was take a couple of tiny samples from a car that only exists today because I died in it. Allegedly, I mean. It's preserved to help us understand the centuries of murder, right? Well, that's what it's doing right now. I'm trying to understand it so that I can stop it from happening again and again. I'm going to end this, Moza. Even if I have to allegedly borrow some tiny samples no one will miss from an ancient car."

"You also exploded all the windows out of a building and caused dozens of injuries."

"Yes. I did do that. Allegedly. But I'm afraid there's no evidence of any of it. You won't find any security footage of the event. You won't find any devices that caused the windows to break. There's not even any evidence I am who you say I am or that I am alive at all. So arresting me won't do us any good. But it will give the serpents time. Time in which they could drop who knows how many more bodies. Time in which they could figure out I'm here and finish the job they started in 2025"

"So give me the story, detective."

I fill her in on everything I know. On the cult and their potential connection to A-S-P. On Manny still being alive and Mary existing at all and the fake IDBs and why we needed samples of the car. All of it. She nods along and sips her coffee and doesn't say a word until it's over. And when it is and I expect her to say, "Okay, you're under arrest whackadoo," she actually says something that rocks me back.

"I pretty much thought it was A-S-P," she whispers. "It all tracks."

"It does?" It's my theory and even I'm only sort of on board with it.

"These people, this cult, they want to shape history, right? That's why they do what they do. They kill undesirables and people who stand in the way of their vision and so on and so forth. They are building the future they want through blood and bone and have done since the dawn of man, basically. This is the logical evolution. You want to control people in this day and age, you control information. You control the internet and movies and books and TV. You control the most powerful corporation in history."

I smile and take a second to gather myself. Something kind of going my way is not a thing I'm used to. "Why haven't you arrested them all? Or at least some of the lower-level guys? Brought them in, put them in the box. Tried to get them to flip?"

"They live on the moon, Khalifa! You do know that, right? Literally everyone you're talking about maybe being guilty lives in a private city they built on the dang moon! That is not just outside of my jurisdiction, it's outside of my planet. My atmosphere. My exosphere!"

"I don't care. They killed my wife. They killed my brother. They killed my partner. I'm taking them down if I have to blow up the whole moon to do it. But I can't do it alone. I need a force. Like a police force." "You need an army," she says. "And you won't find one. The police, the men and women I work with, they're good people. Honorable people. But even if they wanted to help you, and even if we could get to the freaking moon, we're all chipped. And A-S-P can turn us off," she snaps her fingers, "easy as that. We try to stop them and they put us to sleep. Or worse. I don't think the 'malfunctions' are accidents. They're not supposed to be rigged to purposefully explode, but I'm pretty sure they are. Even if we wanted to help, we're no good to you. We'd just be dead in seconds"

"I know that," I say. "That's not the force I'm thinking of. But you can help me get them." So I tell her what I'm thinking. I tell her my plan. And her eyes bulge and I'm pretty sure she's fighting back a laugh.

"When we came here tonight I thought you were crazy. I was wrong. You passed crazy a long way back, Khalifa. You passed crazy doing 180 on the freeway and flipped it off on the way by!"

"I'm not saying you're wrong. I'm just saying, I can get this done. If you do this for me, I can stop an organization that has been murdering people since before we had a word for murder. I can get justice for all of them."

"With this crazy plan you can do that?" she asks.

"I believe in the people of Dubai. Do you?" She thinks on it but not too long. "Yes," she says. "I do. I always have."

"Then trust them. And trust me."

She nods maybe against her better judgment. And she smiles just like Afra used to. She slides a handheld radio across the table to me. "I'm not saying I can get this done," she says. "It's against about a hundred laws and it's dangerous and I may fail. But I'll try. And if I can actually pull it off I will contact you on this to let you know you have a chance. Maybe a snowball's chance in the desert, though."

"A snowball's chance is all I ever needed."

A server approaches the table and hands me a note without once looking at me. "Message for you, sir," he says as he turns and scurries away.

I read the message and I dare to hope for once.

"What does it say?" Moza asks.

"This is from Manny. It's a match. All of it. The steel, the leather, the wood, it's a perfect match for the swords used by the serpents a hundred years ago. I was right. For the first time in history, we know who we're up against. We have a shot."

"So what's next?"

"Well," I say, "I guess I'm going to the moon."

Chapter 27

Getting to the moon isn't as hard as it used to be. Back when I was alive you needed rockets and about a small ocean's worth of rocket fuel. You needed control rooms and engineers and astronauts with seven advanced degrees who trained for years. When I was alive the first time, the only people who ever made it there with boots on the ground were the Americans. It cost them 283 billion dollars to do it. That's in 1960s money. In 2025 money it would have been ten times that. If my math is correct, and it almost never is, that's well over two trillion dollars.

Today they just throw you up there with basically a big pitching machine.

Sounds crazy, right? It is. A bunch of insane people are loaded into a pod, basically just a glass ball a little bigger than a minivan, and the pod is loaded into a vacuum chamber inside a huge machine, a thing like a giant steel disk that stands 40 stories high. An arm inside the machine grabs the pod, whips it around inside the disk fast and faster, not unlike the hammer throw at the Olympics, until it reaches eleven point two kilometres per second, which translates to more than 40,000 kilometres per hour, and then it just spits you out at just the right time and just the right angle. And you are hurled free of the earth's gravity and out into the cold, brutal, terrifying, endless blackness of space.

Escaping the Earth's gravity was always the hard part. Once you're in space you're just sailing through the black at the same speed you left, more or less. Small little thrusters on the pod fire from time to time, adjusting your angle to keep you on target the rest of the 384,472.282 kilometres you need to cross until they go to work slowing you down so that you don't splat like bugs on a windshield when you reach your destination. And then you dock with the moon. The whole journey takes about forty-five minutes these days.

How a human body can be flung that fast without passing out and liquifying does elude me. Manny explained the technology involved that's meant to protect your organs and things and I found myself having a little nap as he did. The point is it works. Apparently.

And we're going to the gosh darn moon.

Hopefully.

Getting there isn't hard anymore. But like all the cool clubs in the solar system, they don't let people like me in the door. And this club is, of course, owned by the evil serpent worshiping cult that I'm trying to tear down with my bare hands. So being allowed into the insane pitching machine thing and then allowed to step foot on the lunar surface, that's going to be the trick. Manny says he has an answer.

"A couple of times a year the powers that be at A-S-P take a few prominent folks up to the moon and show them around and wine them and dine them and do whatever it is ancient murder cults do to see if they're a good fit to become citizens of their weird lunar utopia thing. Notable scientists and athletes and politicians and whatnot are the usual guests. Though certainly they tend to grab the best chefs and architects and things as well. People that they think can build the most perfect future. If the meet and greet goes well they're offered a house on the moon."

"Because that's a thing now. Living on the moon is a thing."

"Yes," Mary says with an eye roll. "Try to keep up, detective caveman."

"It's kind of my fault," Manny says sheepishly. "The same tech that I used to build the Terradome is what they use to encircle the moon. Just super scaled up to give it an atmosphere and breathable air and all the little things people need to not explode in the vacuum of space." "It's cool tech, Manny. You didn't know they'd use it for evil," I say.

"I promise I didn't. And to be fair, they did have to literally kill me to get it from me."

"So back to the people they take up there."

"Right. They take the people they want to craft the future with. And I suppose we can now guess with pretty good confidence that these people are also inducted into the cult we're trying to stop. They only take a small handful of people every year, which makes sense because the moon just isn't that big. The really good news, and I think we can all agree we haven't had enough of that this century, is that it just so happens that they're sending some folk up eight days from now. That's your golden ticket, man," Manny says. "That's how we win."

"You think they're looking to add to their team chain-smoking formerly deceased detectives with self-esteem issues who also want them dead?"

"Seems unlikely. No. But I've got a workaround, bro. They just announced who they're taking up next week. A few scientists and a couple of models because eugenics, I guess. But the key is, Tamir al-Fulan is on the list."

"THE Tami al-Fulan?" I ask with great, mocking enthusiasm.

"Yes!" Manny says, matching my excitement before quickly realizing what's happening. "Oh, right, you have no idea who that is."

"None whatsoever."

"He's the most famous actor in the world today," Mary says. "Also probably the worst. And that's a high, high bar in today's world. Dude is terrible. You know the Razzies? The awards for the worst movies ever year? He won so many that a few years ago they just went on a head and renamed them the Tamirs. So somebody, A-S-P I'd guess, bought the Razzies and shut them down forever."

"Well, if the ancient murder cult also killed the Razzies I guess they're not all bad. What's the point? How does this help me?"

"Tamir is a pretty big guy. Not big like me," Manny says with a chuckle, "but almost your exact height and build. He's like our century's version of The Rock. So, you know, basically your century's version of, I don't know, Keanu Reeves."

I shake my head, obviously still lost. "I can whip up hologram-based disguises no problem. But I can't change your dimensions, right? You're the size you are. I mean, we can give you lifts on your shoes but that's about it. So the couple of ladies who are going up there and the chemist who comes in at a whopping four foot nine inches weighing about 120, they're no help. You're way too big to double them. But I can make your face look like Tamir's, no problem. And of course, I can change your IDB to read like you're him, too. They'll open the door up for you to stroll right in. Because to them, you're supposed to be there. Easy as a lion."

"What happens when two Tamirs show up at the launchpad, though? We just point at each other like the Spider-Man meme and hope for the best?" "Well," Mary says, "Obviously we can't let that happen. So we have to make sure the original Tamir is out of the way for a while."

"So on the heels of my first heist, we're also dabbling in kidnapping folk?" I ask, a little testily.

"Light kidnapping!" Manny protests. "A very surprising vacation basically. We'll put him somewhere nice. Give him everything he wants. He'll send us thank-you cards and maybe an edible arrangement when it's all over probably. It's happened before."

Mary nods. "We still get birthday gifts from that one guy. The pirate we grabbed a couple of years back." "Eddy!" Manny says. "Yes. Good guy. Not a great pirate but hey, it's a tough racket. So what do you say, kyah?"

I put my fist to my chin so it at least looks like I'm thinking really hard. "Even if I look exactly like him, this guy is famous, you said. People will know what he sounds like and how he moves and stuff."

"You've got seven days to watch everything he's ever done and essentially become him, kyah. His mannerisms, his inflections, his syntax, how he holds a glass, what makes him smile and what makes him blush."

Flop sweat immediately drenches me in a way that's never happened any of the thirty-two times someone has pointed a gun at my face. "I have to method act so well nobody knows I'm not really the most famous person on the planet?"

"If you want to save the world then yes," Mary says, enjoying this more than I think is fair.

"Let me tell you about the six different times I played a tree in school plays, Manny!" I shout. "I can't act my way out of a paper bag! There has to be another way."

"I'm a genius," says Manny.

"So am I," says Mary.

"And we haven't come up with anything that resembles a way to get you onto the moon that isn't this. So if you've got a better plan we are all ears. And if you don't…well, my home theatre is pretty sick, bro. We'll load up everything the guy has ever done on film and rock it out!"

I hate this plan so much. But I hate the serpent cult more. They killed my wife and my brother and my partner and kind of me. So I guess I'm about to become an actor. Or die trying.

Chapter 28

These movies are so bad, you guys. Holy crap.

Chapter 29

It should probably be a lot harder than this to kidnap a whole human person.

Maybe it's because there's so little crime here in the future that people aren't vigilant, maybe it's that Manny and Mary are both crazy-smart. Or maybe it's just pretty easy to do terrible things in general and the only reason criminals ever get caught is that they're really bad at crimes. I don't know. But this, so far, is a breeze.

Tamir al-Fulan had a little going away party where a bunch of dead-eyed celebutantes raised a glass of seltzer or milk or human blood, whatever it is these people drink on special occasions, and said 'bon voyage' to the worst actor in history.

In only twelve years he's made one hundred and eighteen feature films. Every single one of them is either overtly or slightly-less-overtly about how corporations are our saviours and the only path forward for humanity. Every single one is worse than the last.

I've seen them all.

In one of the more recent movies, Tamir plays a regular everyday guy who can turn into the superpowered logo of A-S-P, a glass beaker wearing a lab coat and glasses, by saying the company's motto "Science leads the way!" three times in a row.

I actually vomited during that one.

After the party was over Tamir was picked up outside by a very nice limousine where he was supposed to be taken to a very nice hotel where he would rest until morning at which point a giant machine would chuck him into space where he could join a murder cult. As you do.

But this limousine was being driven by Mary. The regular driver will wake up in his own trunk in a few hours a little hungover but otherwise no worse for wear.

When Tamir stepped inside the cabin, he found me waiting for him wearing his face. I expected a scream or something I guess. What I got was more of an "Ooooh."

He gazed at me like he was looking at either his lover or a really good sandwich. "Are you me from the multiverse?" he asked. "I've dreamed of this moment for so long."

Then I'm pretty sure he tried to kiss me which is messed up on several levels.

Luckily, it was right then that a drone about the size of a wasp landed on his neck and injected him with a fast-acting tranquilizer. The same thing we gave the driver.

Tamir will wake up in a safehouse Manny has set aside on the edge of the city where various robots will take excellent care of him for a few days while we go to war on the moon, I'm told.

This was the easiest chance to grab the movie star and transport him to the safe house, and it's hard to argue with the results. But Tamir is expected at the hotel. The staff and a few paparazzi are waiting for his arrival. And if he doesn't show, alarm bells will ring, a search party will be activated, and the lunar launch will likely be scrubbed. So this is my first test as a method actor. I have to be good enough at this role to fool some photographers and bellhops at a billion-star hotel. I have had one full week to prepare. I've watched everything twice, including hundreds of interviews and red-carpet events he attended. I've studied, made thousands of notes about his inflection, his tics, the way he always looks up and to the left when he's thinking, how he says, "well, it's quite interesting actually," when he's trying to buy enough time to think of an answer.

I can tell you he blinks just a little more than the average person, he cracks his knuckles when he's nervous, he sucks on his teeth when he's angry. Something in his left eye bothers him and he rubs it often.

When he uses his fingers to indicate the number two, he always uses his index and pinky fingers, which is frankly silly.

He likes to smell his own mustache.

He uses his lower lip to press his upper lip to his nose and he takes a big sniff fairly often when he thinks no one is looking. Manny got me the same beard oil he uses, because I have to also smell the part, and I have to say it is pretty great. Just a hint of jasmine and honeysuckle.

He walks with a slight hitch in his left hip, an old injury from when he was thrown from a horse as a teenager. They have the technology to fix it now, and he's healed, but his brain has never let go of the limp completely.

I know all of these things and one million other bits of minutia that go into making someone who they are. I know this idiot better than his mother and his wife and his mistress combined.

And my confidence level is this: I'm definitely going to get us all killed. I mean right away. I am going to blow this. No question.

The limo pulls up to the hotel and I take a deep breath.

I check the mirror again. If you've never looked in a mirror and seen someone else's face I do not recommend it. It feels like being unmade. But I have to give Manny credit for the disguise. It works incredibly well. I don't just look like him down to the last freckle. It's not like very good makeup, it's much more. The hologram translates the muscle movements in my face to mimic his. When I smile, the left side of my face appears to rise just a little more than the right, to match his. My jawline could cut glass and my skull appears rounder somehow. My eyes twinkle in a way that only famous peoples' eyes ever seem to twinkle that I still don't understand.

A few more breaths and I'll have the courage to get out of this car, I promise myself.

Four seconds in. Hold for four seconds. Four seconds out. Hold for four seconds. My heart rate slows a little and I struggle to remember it is in fact my heart that's beating. I'm still me. Still Khalifa bin Ahmed. I'm still going to make these monsters pay.

Breath, dummy. You can do this. You're no longer the kid who got fired from the school play for not being good enough at playing a sheep.

I'm just about to open the door when Mary climbs through the little window separating us and into the back seat. She can tell I'm pretty confused. "Tamir is expected to show up with a hottie, detective. And maybe you could use a hand to hold, yeah?" Maybe I could.

"Who's going to drive the car away?" I ask.

"Dad's AI. I already loaded it into the limo's OS. With the tinted windows, no one will know anything is off."

She tears off her chauffeur outfit and there's a ball gown beneath that shimmers like a Christmas tree and hugs her in all the right spots. She can tell what I'm thinking again as I look at it.

"Eyes up, mister," she says.

"Yup."

I slip on a pair of dark black sunglasses even though it's past midnight which makes me feel like an idiot and step out of the car. I'm a star. Stars wear their sunglasses at night for some dumb reason.

I smile a pearly, train-track smile as a dozen flashbulbs go off right in my face. They'd be blinding if I didn't wear the shades. So that's why they wear these things! You really do learn something new every day. I still feel like an idiot.

I take Mary's hand and hear a few "oohs" and "ahhs" and gasps from the crowd. She's wearing the mess out of that dress.

She squeezes my hand just a little to calm me and it works.

Even in the future, pretty girls are magic.

A maitre d'hotel approaches and gestures me forward.

"Right this way, Mr. al-Fulan," he says as we follow him inside. "Your room is prepared just as you always request and the kitchen has already prepared your favorite meal and it is waiting for you."

"Mmmm. Good. Quite right." I say, because that's what his character said to a butler in his eleventh film "Stranger than Normal." It seems to work on the maître d'. Mary smiles. We get on the elevator.

"Well done," she says. "First test passed. Easy as a lion."

"The average person speaks 7,000 words a day. I'm only four in on my first day and I came real close to pooping my pants." She laughs. "Sexy talk really is your forte, detective. Don't ever change."

It feels like another month of flop sweat and nerves before we finally make it inside the room. When we do, I immediately move to turn off the holographic projector making me look like the worst movie star in history. The whole thing is concealed inside of a small gold necklace and all I have to do to deactivate it is hold a certain spot on the chain for three seconds. But Mary stops me.

"Wait," she says with an urgency that ensures I do as she says.

She opens a makeup compact and a swarm of drones, each the size of a dust mote, rises from it and swirls around the luxury suite at speed. Within ninety seconds they've worked their way into every nook and cranny of all three rooms, under the beds and every chair, inside the cabinets and the smoke detectors and the blender and everything else, and returned to the compact in her hand, like a falcon returning to a falconer. "Had to make sure we're clear of cameras and bugs. We are. Place is clean."

I nod and turn off my projector. I immediately pick up a tea kettle with a mirrored surface and make sure I'm still me and I am relieved and maybe even a little surprised to find I am.

"You're doing great," she lies. "It's all going to be fine. We're only saving the world and the future of humanity. No biggie." She gestures to the bedrooms, one on either side of the main room. "Which one do you want?" "You pick. I'm gonna stay out here for a while. I may be too nervous to sleep, honestly."

"Then I'm staying up, too," she says with a smile that's much more kind than I'm used to from her with all of her hard angles and hard words.

I cross to the room service cart in the kitchen where a silver dome covers Tamir's favorite meal.

"What is a movie star's favorite meal, I wonder," Mary says.

"According to six different interviews it is Crayfish, Marrow, Imperial Caviar and Cauliflower Purée served in a poached oyster."

"Sounds disgusting."

"It sure does, I say. Costs about as much as two months' salary for a cop, too."

I lift the serving dome prepared to be horrified and instead I am in awe. I never expected to like anything about this guy, but now I kind of do. Mary can't help but notice the smile.

"What?" she asks, hurrying over.

"Everybody lies, I say."

When she makes it to the cart she can't help but smile, too. And, "Oh my," escapes her lips. "Maybe he's not all bad."

It's not caviar or marrow anything. It's the most beautiful banana split I've ever seen. An entire hand of bananas, a dozen scoops of house-made vanilla ice cream, fresh cherries, freshly whipped cream, and two or three litres of chocolate syrup. The dream food of any toddler or detective.

"Well," Mary says, "I think we have our plan for the evening."

And so we do. We grab two spoons and spend a while eating standing up erupting in little gasps of "Oh yes," and "Mmmm" and things before we drag the cart over to the couch.

As I spoon another gorgeous bite into my mouth I flip on the television, which is just an entire wall, and I laugh so hard I nearly spit a cherry across the room. Of course the first thing I see is "Fury Fingers", my dad's movie.

"What is the deal with this movie?" I ask Mary. "It's everywhere in this ridiculous world." "It's beloved," she says.

"It's terrible!" I counter.

"It is. A bit. Yeah. But it's also great."

I look at her like she's gone completely 'round the bend.

"Look," she says, "It's not just A-S-P. A handful of corporations own everything now. Including art." "You can't own the concept of art," I say.

"You can come pretty close. You can own all the TV stations and movie theatres, book publishers, book shops, museums, galleries, concert halls, and everything else. And when art moves underground, as it did at first, you can buy off the writers and the musicians. And the small few that you can't buy off you can bury in frivolous lawsuits that they can't afford to fight. Nothing is made and nothing is consumed that isn't corporate-approved. That's why all of Tamir's stuff is so awful. It's all made by committee with the express purpose of selling you on their worldview. Their boring, compliant future."

"But your dad's movie sneaked completely under the radar until it was too late. They didn't ban it because nobody watched it. And then it circulated on the grey markets and on late-night screens so slowly that by the time the bosses noticed people were watching it, it was too late to stop it. They tried to take it away about thirty years ago and we rioted."

"This world where nobody will even look anyone else in the eye, stood up and rioted over this terrible film?" I ask.

"We did. It was maybe the last time I was proud of us. Until I met you, at least."

I shake my head, "That's absolutely wild."

"And now it's kind of the one thing we all hold onto. The one thing we all have in common. Your dad is kind of a hero, man."

Without even noticing at first, I start to cry a little at that. "He'd really love that," I say.

"He does. He knows," she says. "He's with you, still. And he's even more proud of what you're about to do. Trust me. I'm a genius."

I wipe away a tear or two and put down the spoon, finally, because my belly hurts worse than I can ever remember. "The human body is not built for this amount of lactose and sugar. I may die," I say.

"What a way to go," Mary says, eating more.

We sit in silence for a few beats as she studies my face. "What is it you're so scared of?" she asks. "Is it the launch? Being off world?"

"Am I scared of being strapped into a minivan and spun around at light speed and kicked to the moon and maybe exploding or liquifying or something along the way? Yeah. I am. But that's the kind of fear I made friends with long ago. That's basically the same fear as a knife in the dark or the barrel of a cheap street gun held on me by a desperate addict. That's the fear I shook hands with every day as a cop."

"So what?"

"I'm afraid of failing. I'm afraid of letting Hanah and Afra and Humaid go without justice. I'm afraid I'm not good enough. That I've never been good enough to stop these people. And it's going to get you and Moza dead."

Mary smiles a sad smile. "We're already dead, detective. This whole world is dead. You've seen it. This isn't living. And if I fall doing this, if I go out trying to make the future a place worth being then I am good with that. My dad was, too."

She gets up and leans down and kisses me gently on the lips.

"Try to rest, detective. Tomorrow we save the whole dang world."

Chapter 30

Honestly, being whipped at the moon in a glass ball and flying through the air at forty-thousand kilometres an hour isn't as bad as I thought it would be.

It's so much worse.

Before the launch, we were given a little safety demonstration, like the "your chair can be used as a flotation device" bit flight attendants always have to before a plane takes off. But this one was a little different.

"On earth, you experience one gravitational force, more commonly known as a 'g-force,' or simply a 'G.' As you move toward Luna today, however, you will experience closer to six Gs. Six sustained Gs can kill a person, but don't worry, it won't last that long and almost nobody dies doing this," the chipper launch attendant announced.

"And those who did die were clearly too weak to live amongst us on Luna, right?"

Everyone cheered and agreed that was correct. Except I was a few moments late agreeing because it's an insane thing to agree on and people did notice something was off. I think that was strike one.

The psychotic stewardess continued, "G-force can have some deleterious effects on even the body of the worthy and chosen, however. The heart can lose its ability to pump blood efficiently; circulation of the blood is then impaired and oxygen is prevented from reaching the brain or other organs sufficiently. This may decrease consciousness. Colors may begin to fade; eyesight may be limited to tunnel vision, and a brief but terrifying blackout may occur.

"In the event of a malfunction that prevents us from reaching escape velocity, prayer is recommended because nothing and no one will stop us from becoming little more than grease stains on whatever part of the planet we crash, explode, and liquify.

"Welcome aboard!"

And with that cheery message delivered, we were off.

Just as promised, we were spun around inside the vacuum tube for several minutes, the speed gradually getting dumber and dumber, until we were flung out the top of the tower and pointed at the moon.

The tunnel vision started coming on hard about halfway through the spin-up. I tried to look at Mary, but we were pulling way too many Gs to move my head.

Amongst all the other forces hammering away at my body, though, I did feel her squeeze my hand again. And, again, it did help. Even for a miserable, dead guy like me, human connection is everything. And it feels utterly lost here.

The A-S-P people seemed pretty surprised when I showed up to the launch with her as my plus-one, but when I told them their options were to let her come up with me or I never again make a film for them, they huddled for a few moments and decided this was fine. We're now about halfway out of the earth's atmosphere and everything is going black.

"Squeeze your abs," a deep, husky voice says. And through the tunnel of mostly darkness, I see Manny sitting in front of me somehow.

I do as I'm told. I squeeze my abs until I think something might pop, and I get back maybe twenty percent of my vision. Which is pretty cool. "I may be hallucinating, but at least my hallucination is helpful," I manage to mostly say through the pain and horror of going to space.

Manny laughs, "I'm not a vision, bro. I'm a hologram, just like always. The projector that makes you look like a movie star also lets you see me. But only you can see me. Don't worry.

"I'm basically in a bowling ball headed toward outer space where I'll try to stop a murder cult. Other people seeing my dead, giant friend is not a worry for me right now.

"Just as I'm about to lose consciousness again, we break the atmosphere. My blood seems to start flowing normally again. I'm weightless.

"And I look down at the blue marble I've spent my life on as it gets smaller and smaller and I start to believe in miracles."

"You're doing great," Mary says.

"I barely survived that."

"Barely is great these days."

I check my surroundings and everyone but me, Mary, and the launch attended are fully passed out. I'm not surprised. Humans have gotten so frail while I was on ice. And these are mostly scientists and two models, one male and one female. Not normally made of the heartiest stock anyway.

They all introduced themselves to me when we arrived but Tamir is too self-absorbed to even notice them, so I didn't either. He doesn't really think of people as people. Just as objects. Some are useful to him like tools so he uses them. Most are things he can ignore until someone less important than him gets around to throwing them away. The more I got to know him the more I realized he was perfect for the serpent cult.

As we continue our path and the moon gets bigger and bigger, most of the other passengers slowly come to. And they look around and down at the Earth as it fades away and they ooh and ahh, too.

Other than those gasps of wonder, though, we all just kind of sit in silence as we float through the blackness of space. We're taking it all in.

Look what we can do.

Humans are capable of anything and mostly we just hurt each other to get things we don't need.

After a while of this, the launch attendant tells us we're making our final approach to Luna, that's what they call the moon because I guess it sounds cooler I don't know.

I feel the thrusters fire a few times rapidly, correcting our course to accommodate for the wind or whatever might have slightly altered our trajectory as we left the earth. And I feel us slow gradually until it feels like we're barely moving at all. And the moon in all her glory is big and bright and just right there and for some reason I want to cry because everything is so magical about this.

There's a whole city up here. Skyscrapers and people and roads and schools and everything. A city on the moon.

Look what we can do.

Then I remember the mission.

A tractor beam grabs us and pulls us toward an airlock and I try to force myself to focus. I think about Hana and Afra and Humaid and everything these monsters have taken from me. There's no problem with blood flow now. It's all headed toward the part of my brain that feels rage and I'm ready.

Manny speaks up again, "If you can get me to any networked computer, I should be able to work my way through the system and do whatever needs doing to expose these people. That's it. That's the mission. Get me to a computer. After that, we should be golden."

I almost answer him but then I remember I'm the only one who can see him and that would make me look crazy. I got away with it once because everyone was almost dead, but now it would just be weird.

As we enter the airlock, one of the scientists has still not woken. I give him a light shake to rouse him, but he's still out cold.

Another shake. More vigorous this time. Another.

He's not out cold.

I check his pulse. My eyes go wide.

"This man is dead," I say.

The launch attendant smiles. She actually smiles. "Good. The selection process is still working. The future belongs to the strong." "To the strong!" Everyone else says in unison.

Everyone but me.

They all look at me. That might have been strike two. Compassion, to these people, is weakness.

One of the models, a man who seems to be made entirely of cheekbones, smiles a sly smile and says, "You're not going soft on us, are you, Tamir?"

And he laughs a little chuckle right up until I punch him in his evil little nose, shattering the bones, squirting blood all over the model to his left, and leaving him unconscious on the floor of our sphere.

"Who's soft?" I ask.

Everyone in the glass ball laughs. Well, everyone who isn't knocked out.

"To the strong," I say with steel in my voice.

Chapter 31

Our pod comes to rest in a sort of airport I guess. It's now a little bloodier than when we left, and there's one fewer living soul aboard.

We're inside the dome, but all around us is just the blackness of space. Stars like you've never seen from the planet. It's a view that was almost worth dying for. But not worth losing my wife for, I remind myself.

A large array of satellite dishes sits just outside on one side of us. That's our ticket. That's how we'll beam back the information that will finally, after hundreds of years, put a stop to the serpent killings. Those little chunks of steel and plastic and circuitry are how I get justice for Hanah, and Afra, and Humaid and the hundreds of thousands of other victims of their sick, twisted mission.

Secrecy has been their most deadly weapon.

The truth is how we win.

Large doors open ahead of us as we step out of the sphere and we are greeted by a terrifying, enormous statue of Buster Guff staring down on us with that poop-eating grin he perfected over a lifetime of smugness and trolling and wealth that could make sultan's blush. This thing is twelve feet tall, muscled like the real guy never was, and kind of green. Like it was made of copper that's gotten a patina of age and wear. It's been up here a while.

You'd expect it to be gold, I think. As expensive and gaudy as possible, but good old buster, that ceaseless self-promoter and grifter went another way. He made himself the new symbol of liberty in the world. That, I feel certain, is where he was going. He's even holding a torch.

I can't wait to find out who's in charge here and punch that guy in the face.

The statue is also kind of bad. Like it was sculpted by a pretty good sculptor, but not a great one, who was working off of heavily airbrushed photos and strict rules to lean toward majesty and away from the truth. This is what you get when you kill all the artists.

I stare at it for a few moments resisting the urge to take a wiz on it. Then the statue moves in a jerky, shuddery way and I realize it's not a statue at all, it's a gosh darn robot. It waves and it tries to smile a robot smile.

"Welcome to your forever home," it says with a voice that's almost but not quite human. And I realize it's the same voice from the drones that tried to kill me as soon as I awoke.

I brush my pocket with my fingers just to reassure myself that the radio Mary gave me is still right where I put it. Maybe it'll never make a sound, but as long as I have it I have a little hope.

A team of dead-eyed ambassadors is standing in a well-rehearsed semi-circle beneath the statue and one of them tells us we should all give ourselves a round of applause for breaking free of the Earth. It's quite the accomplishment to make it to this little heaven they've built with tech they stole from Manny and a dozen other bodies they've dropped, I'm told. We should all be very proud.

They're wearing outfits that look like they're starring in the most expensive Star Trek fan film ever made. Shiny, silver unitard things with a stripe down one side. They even have little rank pips on their collars. It's so dumb.

We all clap for ourselves and how great we are. All of us except the dead guy and the unconscious guy, that is. They've got more pressing concerns.

As we do, a second team quietly takes the body out on a stretcher. Nobody bothers to care that they killed a person.

I can't wait to get out of here, even though I know the only exit for me is probably death.

The head ambassador steps forward a bit and takes the floor. "You all know why you're here. You all know you're worthy. Now just wait until you see the truth about what we have in store for your futures. It is more glorious and it matters so much more than you can know." She turns to me with a smile that's just bad enough that it could have been crafted by the same sculptor who made the robot statue. "Tamir. I hate to ask but I think you all know what we'd like. A little taste of your most famous line, please?"

I laugh as if I'm embarrassed and catch a look at Mary out of the corner of my eye. She's wondering if I know what the heck they want from me. In fact, I'm wondering, too. But I have a pretty good idea.

With my left foot, I slip off my right shoe. And with my right foot, I slip off my left. Mary and Manny are very confused and concerned. But I can tell by the looks on the others' faces that I've got them right where I want them.

I wiggle my toes a little back and forth and shout, "Barefoot on the moon!"

Cheers and applause erupt around the room. That was from Tamir's fourth film, but his first starring role. One of his least terrible (but still truly awful movies) called, "Barefoot on the Moon."

It was just 90 minutes of propaganda about how fantastic Luna is and how jealous everyone should be of the ones who are awesome enough to make it up here. Tamir's character falls in love with the princess of Atlantis in that film, and she offers him a lifetime by her side as the prince and, one day, the king of the underwater utopia, but leaves her to focus on working ninety hours a week as a legal clerk at A-S-P. Because work and only work is what matters in the end if he wants to be barefoot on the moon someday.

Love, happiness, an entire kingdom of wonders are nothing, they tell you, compared to the promise of someday setting foot on their city in the heavens.

As the clapping and laughter fades away Mary breathes a sigh of relief and I suppose Manny would, too, if he breathed.

"Excellent!" the lead ambassador crows. "You're going to be very entertaining here, I'm sure." Her words are dripping so much condescension we're gonna need a janitor in here with a mop. She's so smug she's a slipping hazard.

Oh, I think, *You have no idea how much fun I'm gonna be, lady.*

She asks us to, "Step right this way." She tells us we'll pass through a security door that will scan us to make sure we don't have any contagious illnesses that could spread to the men and women of the moon. If we do, we'll have to be quarantined before we integrate into their golden society.

I give Mary a look and she crinkles her nose to indicate it's nothing to worry about. These are pretty routine in the future, I'd imagine. I trust her and walk through the door.

And that's when the screaming starts.

Chapter 32

And we're running again. I don't even know why this time. But it is what detectives do best.

After the screaming started Mary's eyes nearly bulged out of her head. It all seems sub-optimal.

I don't know if she screamed first or if it was one of the models or all of the ambassadors. It was kind of in unison, I guess. Either way, everybody who wasn't me started screaming and I don't know why.

Then one of the ambassadors punched me in the face.

It felt like somebody's great-grandmother threw a butterfly at me. Still very rude, though. I kicked that guy in the beans and he actually started crying. Made the trip almost worthwhile already.

Then Mary grabbed my hand and yanked me forward while the others mostly kept screaming.

And now we're running.

I can still hear the guy crying in the background and it's still very funny.

"What is happening?" I shout as we tear through the hangar doors and book it down a street that I swear to you is paved with golden bricks, because this place is about as subtle as an orca in your kiddie pool.

"You are you!" Mary yells while yanking me down a side street. Amazing how even on the moon I live my life in alleyways.

"Of course I'm me. Who else would I be? Did everyone have a stroke?"

A slight man in a shiny red jumpsuit pops out of a door in the alley with a gleaming gun in hand that looks just like the one Moza carries. He says, "Say goodnight, Gracie," as he pulls the trigger.

Of course, it does nothing to us since our chips don't have the kill switch in them. So without breaking stride, I tag him in the cheek with a right cross and he crumples to the ground like a sack of laundry. He's out cold before he hits the gold pavement. I say,

"Goodnight, Gracie."

As Mary pulls me through the door the now unconscious guard came from, I just barely have enough to pick up the weapon he dropped. Could come in handy. "No. I mean you're you! Your face. It doesn't look like Tamir anymore. It looks like you! Like Khalifa!"

Well. Crap. Guess that's strike three. The security door that screened for diseases must have deactivated the hologram projector thingy somehow. Maybe the projection read as an illness or something. I don't know. But like I said, sub-optimal.

We sprint through a kitchen where a dozen or so cooks are making something that smells frankly amazing. The future may be mostly evil and terrible, but man can they cook.

Manny appears beside me. "It's okay, kyah. The disguise did its job. It got us on the moon. Get me to a computer and we can end this. Even if we don't survive it, we can end it."

I think we all kind of knew this would be a one-way trip anyway. Maybe I even hoped it would be. When this is done, what's really left for an ancient detective whose wife, parents, and best friend have been dead a century?

Before we left Manny even offered to upload my consciousness to his private cloud servers. So I could live on like he does. But I declined.

I'm old and tired. And I don't belong here. One hundred and thirty years feels like plenty even if I was asleep in a refrigerator for most of them. I'm ready to go. But not before I take these monsters down with me. The cooks all hide and scream some more. I'm getting pretty tired of all the screaming. But I grab a turkey leg on our way through and it really is out of this world. Well...out of this moon, I guess.

We burst through another set of doors and we find ourselves in a lobby. I think this is a hotel where they put visitors who aren't yet citizens of Luna and reporters and folk who aren't part of the cult.

Mary points to the exits and we head that way when a dozen men in red robes and snake masks rush inside blocking the path. I drop my turkey leg.

If we had any doubts that A-S-P and the serpent cult were one and the same I think we can safely lay those to rest.

They're all holding those same swords I saw a century ago. "Dang!" I say. "They mobilized fast!" They hiss.

"Ideas?" Mary asks as we slam on the brakes to avoid impaling ourselves on their blades like horses in medieval war movies.

More and more robed men with snake heads are filtering in all around us, blocking all paths that could lead out of here. We're surrounded. Their swords, I'm sure, are laced with the same vicious venom as before.

One small cut from those blades and we're gone.

Chapter 33

I feel the gun in my hand. It feels like an old friend, but one of those friends you mostly hate.

The creatures in serpent masks hiss some more. Some of them rattle from somewhere or something.

As I stare down the animals who took everything from me, I squint and tap the barrel of the weapon with one finger like a gunslinger because that just feels right.

I'm your huckleberry, I think. *This is just my game.*

Nobody has made a move yet, except to encircle us. Somebody is about to die. I promise myself it won't be Mary.

I hear hissing all around me now. The rattles intensify. Become cacophonous. They drown out every other noise in the room and in the whole world, I think.

I tap the gun. Tap. Tap. Tap.

I can feel my heartbeat in my trigger finger.

"These guys are selected from Earth, right?" I ask. "Not born here?"

"As far as we know," Mary says, looking around for an escape. "Why?"

"So they should have the thing in their heads, right?" Somebody is about to die.

"Oh. Yeah."

I stare at the snakes for another few beats. Their masks make them seem as inhuman as their actions. And I know they can strike as quickly and lethally as the creatures they seem to worship. So I don't give them the chance. I move first.

I say when.

I raise the gun and fire six shots toward the serpents at the main doors as quickly as my trigger finger can pull.

Like watermelons stuffed with dynamite, six heads explode in front of us one after the other. Pop pop pop.

It's a geyser of red and grey.

It's gallons and pounds and nightmares worth of liquids and semi-solids on the walls and the floors and on us.

I didn't see that coming.

"Sweet mother of mercy!" Mary yells.

All the other serpents run away, diving behind things for cover or just hightailing it out of here as fast as they can slither.

I spin, my gun still raised, taking in the room. Making sure nobody tries for our blindside.

We're clear.

I've kept my promise. For now.

Mary grabs my hand once again and yanks me toward the doors.

We have to leap to hurdle the headless bodies.

When she lands, Mary slips on some blood and brain matter. She falls fast toward the steel coated in snake venom.

One scratch is all we need for this to have all been in vain. One scratch and the future is doomed.

I throw out my hand and catch her flailing arm before she hits the ground. I squeeze so hard I see her wince and grit her teeth.

She looks down to see how close she was and "close" doesn't begin to describe it. She was centimeters, maybe nanometres from one of the blades.

"I can actually smell the venom," she says.

I pull her back to her feet.

And we run.

We have no idea where anything or anyone is on this forsaken satellite. Everything is alien. Everything is potentially deadly. So we just run for a while. A few blocks down, ten, maybe a hundred I'm not sure, we stop for a beat. No one seems to be chasing us. I still have the gun and nobody wants to be the next to lose their skull. They're regrouping or plotting or something. I'm sure we'll find out. I'm sure it will be unpleasant to live through it. But I promise myself we will. Until Hanah is avenged, I will live through anything.

Mary ducks behind a corner and takes a moment to vomit.

"You okay?" I ask knowing neither of us are okay and maybe never have been or will be.

"I just need a sec," she gasps between heaves.

"I didn't know their heads would…you know. I thought it would just stun them," I offer. I don't know why.

"Well clearly it wasn't," she says.

"Yeah. Clearly."

I'm not sorry.

I fiddle with the weapon a little until I find a switch near the trigger that, I assume, cycles between safety, stun, and head explosion settings. I leave it on "head explode." "They'd have done the same to us," I say. I don't have time to mourn monsters today.

"I know. I'm good." She wipes her mouth. "We need a plan and, if possible, so very much mouthwash."

"Manny," I say and he appears in front of us. He takes a few beats to look at his daughter on one of the worst days of her life and to hate that he can't hold her. He takes a beat to remember that he's dead and it breaks my heart.

"Yeah, bro," he finally says. "That was real messed up back there! Not cool at all."

"It was. But we need to focus, yeah? We can still make this work. The three of us can do this."

"Yeah, bro. Hundred percent. What do you need?" "Toothpaste and a new tongue!" Mary quips.

"Can they track our chips? Know where we are?" I ask.

"Nah, bro. I turned the IDBs off completely once you were found out. Just in case. You're invisible to that tech. But not to cameras and, you know, eyeballs obviously."

"Good," I say. "Then we just need to get somewhere they can't get a visual on us."

"Won't be easy," Mary says. "This place is covered in CCTV. And they've already got drones in the air, I'm sure. Those will have cameras and guns and they won't have chips to make their heads explode. And we're all out of duct tape"

I look around for some way to disappear for a bit where the drones won't find us and, like Dorothy and the Tin Man, I find my path on the yellow brick road. I point to it. "There's a manhole. We go underground. The sewers."

"So I can add pee and poo to the list of bodily fluids I'm soaking in? This day is the worst."

"I'm open to other ideas," I say. But Mary knows there aren't any coming anytime soon. She's already got the cover off the manhole and she's climbing inside.

"You coming?" She asks.

Yeah. I'm coming.

Chapter 34

Even on the moon in the future, everybody poops.

Even members of a murder cult that predates history need to go potty.

If you want to have a city, you have to have a way to process waste. And that means having a way to move around under a city, which is useful if you're an incredibly desperate detective on a mission to avenge your dead wife and save the planet.

Or a teenage ninja that happens to also be a turtle.

What you don't have to do, I guess, is have lights down in those. It's blacker than pitch in here and I don't know what I'm standing in but there's almost no chance I'm happy about it.

"Do you have any light?" I ask Mary even though I'm pretty sure I know the answer.

"No." She says. "But I can see in the dark. I had the surgery a few decades ago. Implants that take any available light and read it well enough to see virtually anywhere. Even down here there's enough illumination just from the LEDs on the control boxes every few meters to see fine. I can guide you if you hold my hand."

Manny pops up again and says, "No need to cuddle. I got you guys." And suddenly a powerful blue light erupts from my necklace illuminating the entire tunnel. "Holograms are just light, my man. Instead of using it to make an image, I can focus it into a beam."

I take a beat to look around. It's pretty darn nice down here. For a sewer, I mean. The walls are ornately tiled, like the walls in a bathroom at a restaurant with at least one Michilin star. Everything glistens because it's all practically brand new.

Waste is flowing at a consistent pace at our feet, but it's not rushing like a river. It's not deep. We can do this.

"I'm guessing if we follow the current," Mary says, covering her nose and mouth with her sleeve to block the stench, "we'll end up at a treatment plant that converts urine to water. They built a few lakes and things up here on the surface if you can believe it. It rains inside the dome and whatnot. But water is still hard to come by in space, no matter how rich you are." "What good does a treatment plant do us?" I ask. For the one hundred billionth time since I've met her,

Mary looks at me like I'm an idiot. "Those processes have got to be controlled by computers, right? We get to one of those machines and dad can do his thing. Infiltrate the network. Get all the dirt we need to expose these maniacs to our people and world governments and whatnot."

"Make sense," I say, hoping it's not far a walk.

The moon is bigger than you probably think. Nearly 3,500 kilometres in diameter. About a quarter the size of the earth. At average walking speed, it would take about a year and a half to walk the whole thing. So it's pretty big.

The city that these monsters want to build will cover the entire thing if we let them. But it doesn't yet. So far it's only about ten kilometres across. Still, that's ten kilometres more than I want to wade through urine and faeces.

We march in silence for a while. We're both about to die and I just killed six men a few minutes ago. It's something you need to sit quietly with for a bit, I guess. But I worry if we linger on it too long we may be paralyzed by the horror or the totality of it all. PTSD is for after the trauma. We can't afford it during the trauma. So I decide to ask a question that should dig right into the center of her big, nerdy brain and get her talking about something else.

"Why aren't we floating?"

It takes her by surprise. "What?"

"Not floating. Not zero gravity but bouncy, I guess. Like the old videos of the American astronauts. Why aren't we bouncy? The moon's gravity should be half or a third of Earth, right? But this feels the same as ever." "The moon's gravity should be one point six two meters per second per second," she says knowing full well that won't mean anything to me.

"Oh. Of course." I say.

She laughs a little which I choose to believe is a good thing. Her mind is leaving the darkest place I think.

"It's about a sixth of the Earth's gravity. Which is nine point eight zero seven meters per second per second," she says just to show off.

"Right. Obviously," I say. And I get another chuckle. "So why aren't we floating?"

We both hop over something flushed by a person who clearly had a heavy, potato-based diet I'd guess. "They made some gravity."

"Why would they do that? Moon gravity sounds awesome! It would be like living your whole life on a trampoline. Imagine how good basketball would be on the moon? Slam dunks from half-court on a net fifty feet in the air! Six somersaults on your way to the rim! Man, these guys ruin everything fun."

Mary smiles and her eyes twinkle a little and I think maybe she's going to be okay. "Maybe the most dangerous thing about living in space is the lack of gravity," she says. "For one thing, it plays merry hell with your bones. You lose about one and a half percent of your bone density for every month you're in space. Stay long enough and your bone density gets to a place where they're not so much bones anymore. More like, I don't know, pudding. Or flan."

And just like that I'm never eating flan again. "A lot of the bone loss is from calcium leaking from them. But the calcium doesn't just disappear or evaporate or something, it flows through your system until it turns into kidney stones. You ever had a kidney stone? They say the pain of passing one is worse than giving birth. Another issue is that gravity keeps our blood pressure where it's supposed to be, much greater in our feet than in our brains. Take gravity away and blood pressure equalizes all over your body, raising it in your brain by a significant amount. That can lead to strokes and blindness and always leads to your face plumping up with fluid. Everyone is uglier in space. Your heart also just kind of withers on the vine because it has so much less work to do, because it's not fighting gravity. Just kind of shrivels up after a while. Your heart is a pretty important organ. There's more but I think you get the idea."

"Yes," I say. "Got it. Space wants us dead."

"It sure does." "Isn't that all maybe worth it for how funny sports would be, though?"

She rolls her eyes, but I can tell she's thinking about how awesome it would be.

"But how did they just make gravity?" I ask, both to keep her talking and because I'm genuinely curious.

"Essentially," she says, "As crazy as it sounds, they drilled to the core of the moon and created a tiny, super dense, artificial star there."

"We can do that?"

"They can. Apparently. Honestly the science on that is beyond me and dad both."

Manny pops up to defend himself. "Just because I haven't figured something out doesn't mean I won't," he says kind of in a huff. It's adorable.

"The star is about the size of a softball, I'm told. But it's so dense that it creates the extra pull to get the moon to essentially the same gravitational force as the Earth." "That's crazy! How does it not just melt the moon? Those things are pretty hot as I understand it."

"It's suspended in a containment field," she says, "But that's definitely a concern should the field ever fail. Interestingly, that little ball of burning plasma is also what powers the moon. The entire city runs off that one itty bitty star."

The things we can do, man. And we use our gifts for murder cults and bad films.

And then she stops moving. She studies the walls high above us for a bit. "These aren't just sewers," she says. "This is also a utility tunnel. It's carrying the city's electrical grid." She stands on tippy-toe and runs her hand along some of the cables lining the tunnel. "And it's all pouring into something above us. Could be offices or an indoor park or something."

"That means there are a lot of people up there, probably," I caution. "Yeah," she says. "But it also means there will be computers up there."

I stare up at an access hatch for a little too long, trying to game out something with a hundred million variables I can't begin to fathom.

"What's the matter, detective?" Mary asks, reading the concern on my face. "You wanna live forever?"

Chapter 35

We climb.

We climb up the ladder.

We climb into hell.

Manny tells us to stop just before we breach the hatch leading out of the tunnels. We're close to a camera signal, he says. He can feel it in his digital bones or something. And he can piggyback off of it just enough to look around. See if the coast is clear. See how much resistance we're going to face.

See if someone else is about to die.

After a little while he tells us, "Everything up here is automated. No guards to worry about. But…oh. Oh no."

"What's the matter?" I ask.

"Hang on." He doesn't say anything and we don't move for seconds that feel like years. Finally, he speaks again. "The cameras can't get me into any sort of central terminal. They're not networked to anything except monitors. I can loop them so nobody watching them off-site knows you're here but…maybe we should just move along. Find another hatch. Another building."

"Is there likely to be a computer up there that works," I ask, confused by a side of Manny I've never seen.

"Yes. Probably. But—"

"Then this is a bird in the hand. A bird that's not currently surrounded by killer snake people. Who knows what happens at the next building? Who knows if we even make it to the next building alive? Not to be dark but—"

"Yeah, bro. Yeah," Manny says. "I get it. Give me two minutes to loop the footage and cover our tracks. Use the time to pray, maybe."

We do as we're asked. We wait. And we say a few prayers for whatever is up this hatch. The not knowing has to be worse than whatever it is though. Right? After all we've been through, what could possibly shake him like this?

When Manny gives us the go-ahead, we climb.

It takes a few seconds for it to sink in. It takes a bit for me to be able to fathom the depravity and madness I'm surrounded by. I was wrong. Not knowing was better. "I'm sorry," Manny says like it's his fault. Like he didn't die trying to fight whatever this is.

The room is huge. It's a warehouse of fifteen or twenty thousand square meters at least. And I don't think this is the only room in whatever building we're in. "Mother of mercy," Mary says, taking it all in but not processing what's in front of her. Not really. Not yet.

The only things in the room are glass pods, roughly shaped like eggs, each connected to dozens of wires and tubes and things. Each egg is filled with some sort of viscous, amber-colored liquid not unlike clean motor oil. And in each egg is a person.

Thousands, probably tens of thousands of people.

I wander row after row of pods fighting the urge to vomit. Fighting the urge to figure out a way to nuke this entire place.

The people in the eggs range from maybe thirty or forty to two or three years old. All of them on breathing machines, none of them intact.

They don't have names.

They're numbered.

Some people are missing eyes and ears. Some are missing limbs. Most are missing huge patches of skin. All of them have stitches running all across their naked bodies. Especially where the important organs are located. I know the kind of incision you make to remove a gallbladder by heart at this point. I see a lot of those cuts.

"What is this place?" Mary asks, utterly lost. She's older than me, but much more naive. Manny raised her not to be a miserable pile of crap and splinters like her friend the detective.

She looks around a little more. "Is it some kind of hospital?"

"No." I say. "It's a farm."

Chapter 36

Mary wants to blow up the whole dang moon now. I get it. I do. This is grotesque. It's unthinkable. Unforgivable. It's a violation of everything we're supposed to hold dear. It feels worse than just murder, somehow, even though the end result is the same. But I don't think her solution is sustainable.

"I don't even care if we get off the surface at this point. But screw exposing them or whatever. We just blow them all to the afterlife which is a place I can guarantee they will not enjoy!"

"I feel you," I say. "I do. But I don't think there's a self-destruct button for the moon."

"There's the star!" she shouts with genocide in her eyes. "The star at the center of this crap heap creating the extra gravity. We could turn off the containment field. It would implode and burn the moon in seconds!" "I like your passion, Mary. But there are a lot of problems with that."

"Like what? I'm a genius and I don't see anything wrong with exploding every single one of these monsters! And no offense but you're basically a half evolutionary step up from a bag of hammers. I mean you're cuter but brain-wise…"

"Well, for one," I say ignoring the hurtful and probably true statements about my brain, "if we commit genocide, even against bad people, I think that makes us pretty bad people. Two, the cult will rebuild. There's no way this is all there is. They have plenty of agents on Earth. We know this because they're killing people down there right now by the hundreds. And perhaps most importantly, I think the moon is pretty important for life on Earth."

"They'd be fine probably! They'd figure it out."

Manny pops up again. "Sweetie," he says, "the detective is right. Without the moon, the tides would collapse which would lead to the mass extinction of ocean life. Which would lead to mass extinction of the animals that feed on those animals. Which would lead to mass extinction of the animals that feed on those.

And so on. And the moon stabilizes the tilt of the earth. Without it, seasons would become bananas erratic. Regular Ice Ages would occur which would lead to…"

"Mass extinction. I get it. The moon is important. Screw both of you guys. I just want to hurt them."

"We will," I say. "I promise. I promise you and Hanah and everyone. We are going to make these animals bleed. We'll turn their evil empire to ash."

"Speaking of which, let's find a computer, yeah?" Manny says. "So I can do what I do best: crimes!"

Manny is infectious and that makes us smile despite being surrounded by horror like nothing any of us have ever conceived.

A quick jog around the room revealed nothing but the eggs, so I took the first door I came to which led to a hallway. I took the first door again and found a bathroom, which was great because I really needed to pee.

One bathroom break and two rooms later I found a control room with about a dozen computers in it. It also had a dozen monitors showing a dozen more warehouses the same size or bigger. The body farms seem endless. I ignore it for now because that's all I can do without losing it.

"Bingo," I said.

Manny appears once again from my necklace and immediately finds a way to wirelessly insert himself into the machine.

"Is this really about to be over?" Mary asked. "With a little luck, yes," I say. "He should be able find records of murder and who knows what else going back centuries. And the satellite array outside can beam them directly to every news station and straight into every home and office and saloon on the planet. We can do this."

The various computer screens go wonky, flickering and rapidly cycling through files and folders and things. It's all working faster than my eyes can follow, like an entire film shown in a single second. And despite all that speed, it takes forever.

"Maybe we can wake them up?" Mary says, staring at the monitors, a few rivers of tears streaking her face. "Maybe they can be saved."

"Maybe they can," I say. "But not by us." She looks at me pleadingly. "Almost all of them are missing vital organs, Mary. If we take them out of their stasis eggs or whatever, they'll die. If we do this right, though, if we take these people down and we get decent humans up here with an army of crazy-good doctors, then maybe, maybe, maybe a lot of them can be saved. But none of that can happen if we don't finish the mission. You understand? We have to do what we came here to do. No cracking up now."

"I'm good," she says, a little of the old edge working its way into her voice. "We're going to make them pay." I nod.

We wait some more.

Tom Petty was right. Waiting is the hardest part.

Manny is gone for fifteen, maybe twenty minutes. An eternity when you're this close to your goal of avenging your wife and an entire moon worth of snake people want you dead.

My mother always said patience was a virtue.

I've never felt too virtuous.

Eventually, he resurfaces with a look on his enormous, powerful face that I've never seen before. If I had to guess I'd say he's…embarrassed.

"So I've got bad news and I've got worse news," he says with a cringe.

"What did you do, dad?" Mary asks with a tone of disappointment so withering it could kill a garden.

"The bad news is this computer is no longer connected to any sort of network. If I had to guess I'd say they basically turned off the internet for the moon when we got found out. Which I realize is at least partly my fault as well. I did try to find some back doors or some way to reconnect but it's not happening. We're essentially air gapped."

"So we can't access what we need from here?" I ask, dreading whatever comes next.

"We cannot. We also probably cannot from any other random computer. We're going to need to get to the server room, I'd imagine. Which, one assumes, will be pretty heavily guarded at this point. That's the bad news."

"What's the worse news?" Mary asks.

"The worse news is that I believe, in my digging around, I have set off several booby traps and the baddies pretty definitely know where we are. And they're coming to kill us. Immediately."

"That'll do for worse," I say.

And then someone starts trying to knock down the doors.

Chapter 37

"I do have some good news," Manny says. "Or potentially worse news, from a certain point of view." Another bang at the door.

I'm on the moon, surrounded by some kind of sick, twisted living body farm and a prehistoric murder cult knows where I am, they're right outside the door, and they're very motivated to kill me. Worse wouldn't have seemed physically possible a hundred years ago. Today it feels like standard operating procedure. "I don't want riddles or cuteness, Manny. What do you have?"

Another bang and a scream from outside. Someone's frail future body breaks against the door. Even as weak as these snakes are, they've got the numbers. They'll get through soon enough.

"I found our way out."

"How is that worse?" Mary asks with appropriate urgency coursing through her voice.

Bang!

Bang!

Bang!

"It's…" Manny grimaces.

Bang!

"There's a chute. A thing they use to dump the bodies that are no longer viable."

Mary vomits again. I don't blame her.

"Show me," I say.

Manny points to one of the monitors. In the far corner of the room we just came from is a small square hatch,

I guess you could call it. It's big enough for a human because it's built for our bodies. Bang!

"That's our best bet?" I ask.

"Best I can see, kyah. And—"

"Fine." I cut him off. I can't bear to hear how he's a genius one more time. I take Mary by the hand and I run.

Bang!

Bang!

Crack!

The door is giving way.

We sprint.

I reach the hatch first and open it. I motion for Mary to dive in. She stops.

"I can't," she says. And I know she's telling the truth. She's frozen. And I don't have time for it. I pick her up bodily and chuck her down the chute before following her in.

He who hesitates is lost.

We slide maybe three stories and land hard. I expected to land in water. Or not water but whatever that amber-colored liquid is that fills the eggs. Some kind of artificial amniotic fluid or something. Or maybe it's not artificial. That's a terrifying thought, but they're farming everything else up there.

But instead, I land in a pile of ash maybe a meter deep. Immediately, Mary and I are completely covered in shades of grey. I guess that's appropriate. I understand what's happening as soon as I hit. Mary needs a second.

"What…why would…no…this is just a trash chute," she says. "That's not so bad."

She chooses not to believe it or recognize it and I let her. I'll never tell her what she already knows. That we're in a cremation chamber. And maybe one day, if she survives, she'll actually believe this is just for waste paper and things.

Faintly I hear the echo of another crack and a crash upstairs. They're through the doors. I hear voices shouting and footfalls as they search. I hear one of them figure it out. "They're in the furnace!" he shouts.

"Run," I whisper.

And we do.

The furnace is the size of a classroom and Mary is out the door just as the first snake lands in the ashes behind us. He stands and we stare at one another for a moment. I try to see humanity behind those eye slits and I find none. He raises his sword and he sprints toward me.

"Let's go!" Mary shouts.

I turn and dive toward the exit.

Mary slams the heavy steel door behind me, but the snake gets a hand into the doorway. The door bounces off his hand. It can't latch shut.

The steel shatters every bone in his hand and he screams bloody murder but he doesn't pull back.

Through the paperback-sized gap that remains, I see another snake slide into the furnace. And another. And another.

Mary pushes with all her might against the serpents trying to open the door. She may be hot but she's Manny's kid. She's as strong as three of them.

There are at least four pushing against her, though, so I join in putting my shoulder to it.

I hear another fifth, sixth, and seventh snake slide down and run and grunt as it pushes, too.

I'm stronger than maybe four of them combined but it's just a matter of time. Of very little time. We are going to lose this fight.

And then, just about within arm's reach, I see the button.

Mary sees me see it and it's awful and the look we share says we both know just how awful it is. And she nods at me. And I nod at her. And with one hand still fighting with all my might to keep the door from opening, to keep certain death a few feet away, I stretch.

I stretch and groan and grimace to the point that I think my arm might just come out of its socket. And I make it. I hit the big red button.

And inside the furnace, the flames roar to life.

And the snakes scream and hiss and burn alive.

And I know they're the bad guys. I'm just not sure if I'm still one of the good ones. Maybe I never was.

I am covered in them. Shades of grey.

Chapter 38

As ever, there was no time to mourn or think about what we'd just seen and done. We had to move. They'd find another way to our location and be on us in no time. So, as ever, we ran.

"There is some good news," Manny said. "Actual, not rolling around in...well, good news."

"I'll take anything."

"I got us a map. Stole it off the computers in the last room."

And a holographic map pops up in front of me, like a heads-up display. It even has a little version of me running on it, showing my location as I move through the streets like it's Google Maps or something.

"And," Manny says, "I know where the server room is. I've mapped the optimal route to get there with maximum cover to avoid drones and snakes."

"Always impressive, my friend," I say, still running, only now following the path illuminated before me by Manny's map.

We stick to side streets, take cover in trees and bushes and under park benches and storefront awnings, and at one point in a dumpster for more than an hour. We watch roving bands of single-minded killers searching for us until the coast is clear and we can run once again.

Rotting trash smells just as great on the moon in the future as it does everywhere else.

We move like secret agent cats trained by Batman. Melting in and out of shadows, with Manny peeking around corners and taking over security cameras when needed.

All told, it takes us just over four hours to make it about three-quarters of a kilometre. But make it we do. And now we're standing in the server room containing thousands of years of proof and evidence that should be enough to cripple the most evil organization in history.

Mary attaches what looks like a refrigerator magnet to one of the servers and explains that this is actually a little machine that will rip every piece of data, download it to the magnet, and stream it directly to the satellite array outside to be transmitted back to earth and onto every television, computer, phone, and refrigerator in the world.

"What if they turn off the internet here?" I ask. "Won't that keep us from sending it?"

"Doesn't matter," Manny says. "I can just turn it back on from here. This is where everything is controlled. Including the satellite dishes you see right outside the window. We're in control of the whole operation."

I take a moment to stare at the fifteen enormous satellite dishes outside. It's appropriate, I think, that they look like shields to me. That they look like a phalanx. We're going to use them to protect the future.

"And people will actually see it?" I say, asking a question that probably should have occurred to me before now. "A-S-P won't be able to block it or censor it?"

"They own the internet," Mary explains, "But they operate it from here. So we own it now. We can send it directly to every device on the planet and there's nothing they can do to stop us, because we've got the hardware. The only way to prevent us from sending this now would be to—"

And that's when the entire array of satellites outside the window explodes.

"Would be to do that," Mary says.

Chapter 39

Okay. Time for Plan B.

"We have a Plan B, right?" I ask the lady and the holographic ghost who can't stop telling me how genius their geniusing always is. They just stare at me like lost puppies. "We maybe use some kind of satellite internet. Buster Guff had that working a hundred years ago so surely—" Mary just shakes her head.

"That was turned off decades ago."

"So we turn it back on. Manny said we controlled the internet from here so—"

Manny says, "The satellites' orbits degraded and fell back to Earth ages ago. We don't control time travel or physics,"

"I time traveled!" I shout, getting angrier and more desperate than I'd like. "Maybe I took the long way 'round, but I basically teleported through a hundred years of horror and lost everything I ever loved so I'm not accepting that this is just over!" I tear the data ripper thingy from the server and hold it high in my fist. "We have come too far. We literally have the information in hand. I'm not losing to these monsters. So what is our Plan B?"

Mary shakes her head. "We have to physically deliver the data We need to get back home."

"Every single person on this moon wants to stop us, wants to kill us, and we have to steal a spaceship that we probably don't know how to drive, fly it nearly 400,000 kilometres through a vacuum, navigate to the right city on the planet, and land it safely back home without dying or losing the data?"

Mary nods, "Yes."

I smile. "Piece of cake."

Manny projects an image of the server contents in front of us and starts zipping through some files he pulled off the thing. "It's actually not as bad as all that, kyah. I've got an autopilot program here. It'll do all the flying and navigating for us. We just have to get to a ship."

I flip up a monitor from a nearby server and find the security feed from the airport thing where we arrived. There are, best guess, around seven thousand people in there. All in snake masks. All holding swords. All ready to kill us. "Looks like they figured out our Plan B before we did," I say.

Manny keeps zipping through files at lightning speed. Soon he pauses and chuckles. It's a welcome sound, like cannon fire from an army sent to rescue you. "There's a private hanger not far from here. A single ship. It's through a secret tunnel leading away from what looks like the office of whoever or whatever is in charge. Probably very few people know about it, because it's probably meant to give him an escape route that would leave his followers to die in case of an emergency. Like if they're ever invaded or the gravity star fails or something. I only found it because these ghouls are still using the code they stole from me for everything, so I was able to walk through their security. If we can get there, I think we can maybe get off this rock alive."

Plan B just started to sound like an actual plan.

Manny uploads a map to my heads-up display.

"We do this and maybe we actually get to see who's in charge of this thing," I say. "And punch him in the nuts." That gets a pretty good laugh.

We all forget that this is insane and will never work and we're definitely all going to die.

"You really think we can do this?" Mary asks. "I do," I say. "I have faith. For maybe the first time since well before I was frozen, since before my wife died, even, I have faith." "Me, too," Mary says.

"Me, three," Manny says.

We take a moment to rest in the knowledge that we do actually believe in one another. We believe that a small band of bat-crap crazy believers on a mission to do good can actually change the world and the future forever. Because it's the only thing that ever has.

We take a moment to do the most daring thing a human can do in this day and age: to hope.

And then we get to work.

Now that he's plugged into the central server, Manny has more control than ever before over the systems around us. Before he could really just observe, now he can act in a host of ways.

He can lock and unlock doors, feed false information to terminals and handheld devices, and set off dummy alarms anywhere on the moon to draw people away and confuse them.

Anytime a commanding snake sends an order to anyone to do anything, Manny intercepts it first and changes the message, confounding their security endlessly.

He does a great job clearing a path to the offices of the Moon President or whatever the motherless monster running this crap show calls himself. But still, we take it slow like you mean it.

We crawl through air ducts and we hide in closets and jump in and out of windows and I still have the gun, which comes in handy a few times. Though I did set it to stun now for better or worse.

Soon enough we make it to the offices of their ruler. The head snake. It's guarded by ten serpents. I take them all out with the pistol before they have time for a single pitiful hiss.

The tech they've used to control the world for decades is their undoing. It's delicious.

Before I walk inside, Manny says to wait. It's essentially a huge panic room. It's the most secure place on the moon. Manny has the keys, of course, but he just wants to prepare me. He's in there. The king snake.

"Who is it," I ask. "What's his name?"

Manny keeps zipping through files. "I can't find anything on the server. It's a complete secret, even from the higher-ups. It's bizarre but I'd guess almost no one even in the cult knows who's really leading this thing. That's why they still have Buster Guff as the face of it, I guess."

In a way that makes it more exciting. Like unwrapping the best birthday gift of all time.

We're finally going to know who's behind this.

"Is anyone else in there?" I ask.

Manny shakes his head. "I don't know. No IDBs are pinging, but that's all I can say for sure. If any of these people were trusted enough to not have the chip…"

"Well," I say. "Let's find out."

I try to imagine the face of the man that can do all the things this creature has done. And all the faces of the countless leaders before him who have murdered and terrorized their way to this horror show future. And I can't do it. I can't come up with an image that fits something that insanely, grotesquely evil.

Let's find out.

And a hundred years of anger and hate and hurt boils inside of me. I can't wait to hurt this monster. I won't use the stupid shiny gun. I won't speak. I'll hit this creature until my hands break and his face liquifies and I'll laugh the whole time.

I hear dozens of locks disengage and twist and pull back as Manny opens the room.

I pull on the heavy steel door and swing it away from the frame like accessing a bank vault.

And I storm inside ready for war.

And then I see the king snake.

I see that he is a she. A queen snake, instead.

She's looking out the window, her back to us. And then she turns.

And my blood runs cold. And my heart nearly explodes.

And my knees go weak.

"Hello, Khalifa," says the queen snake. "I've been expecting you."

And I shed a single tear.

Because I'm staring at my wife.

Chapter 40

I can't move. Can't breathe. The only thing I can say is, "Hanah?"

You'd think nothing could shock me at this point. You'd be wrong.

Manny gasps.

"Who's Hana? Why are we…oh no!" Mary says.

Hana smiles. A smile that could launch a war in any century. And has.

She's as old as me. 130, give or take. And somehow she looks younger than when she died.

After what seems like an eternity I manage one more word. "How?"

Asking "why" matters a lot more, but I'm not ready for that conversation yet. I know somehow that I'll really never be ready for that.

The way she holds herself, the way she moves, the way she breathes, even, I remember it all. For most of my life it was my whole world.

I remember so much. And I am so lost. And so scared. I didn't know I could still be scared like this. "I know you must have so many questions, dear," Hanah says with a cruel edge in her voice that I also remember well. "Unfortunately, husband, I'm afraid you're about to be hit in the face by an enormous robot."

And that's when I get hit in the face by an enormous robot.

Chapter 41

I've been punched in the face by seventy-three men, five women, eighteen dogs, and a gorilla named "Chauncy" once. None of them hit this hard. It's the robot of Buster Guff. Or it's one just like it. Twelve feet tall and copper. Copper is not the hardest metal, but it's hard enough when a fist the size of a medicine ball catches you in the eye socket and rockets you into a wall.

The broken bones in my face don't hurt quite as much as the sound of my dearly departed bride giggling about it all, though.

I don't have time to deal with the frankly very complicated emotions surrounding that right now. If I don't figure something out in a hurry, I won't have any more time at all.

I didn't even notice the dang robot was in the room. I was too busy staring at my long-dead wife who is apparently the head of a cult that has been murdering people since before we had words for "cult" and "murder" in any language.

The robot is fast. Faster than something this huge and ancient-looking should be.

After I bounce off the wall, I collapse to the ground. I have just enough time to gather my limited senses and roll to my left before the copper con man stomps me into a puddle.

The floor is steel, several feet thick, and it bends a little under the stomp.

I run.

It chases.

I keep moving around the perimeter of the room. I could probably make it to the door, but then it would just turn its terrible attention to Mary. There's no way she gets past it alive.

So I just keep moving.

As long as it's after me it's not after Mary.

"You'll tire before Buster does, love," Hanah says.

"So…why didn't your marriage work?" Mary asks. I duck and dive out of the way of a haymaker.

"Oh, she's funny. I like watching the funny ones die best," Hanah says. "They're never laughing in the end."

I get a heavy wooden desk between me and the bot. It's made of axe breaker wood, I think. Maybe it'll slow things down. "Manny!" I yell. "Can you take this thing over, please? Like all the other electronics in here?"

We circle the desk slowly, the murder bot and me. It's playing with its food.

"Who in the world is Manny?" Hanah asks. "Are you delirious already? I thought you were made of sterner stuff, love,"

"Sorry, kyah," Manny says. "This tech is old. Ancient. Close to a century out of date, brother. You'd need ancient tech to hack it. I don't have the right tools. I'm so sorry, bro. You're on your own."

Well, at least I'm used to that, I guess. It tosses the desk aside like an empty box of tissues. The desk splinters against the steel wall.

I throw a hard right cross to Buster's dumb grinning face and only succeed in breaking a few more of my bones.

He clocks me in the side and I feel two ribs go as I run again.

"Let's see who laughs in the end, psycho lady!" Mary yells as she dashes for a splinter the size of a chef's knife.

But before she can reach it, a dozen snakes march into the room and surround Hanah.

"It was a trap, of course, husband. And not even a hard one to see coming. If you have half a brain. You never did have half a brain."

I can't run anymore. Too many things are broken.

"I'd like to say I'm sorry to have to kill you," my wife says, "but mostly I'm just sorry it didn't take the first time I did it."

The huge statue of one of the worst people to ever live corners me. It clamps a massive hand around my throat and lifts me off the ground.

Hanah moves closer. "Do it slow," she says. "I want to watch the light in his eyes go out."

Things start to get a little dark—my vision tunnels. My head feels light.

And then my stomach starts to get hot.

It feels like it's turning over and over.

Am I going to vomit on the way out? I always thought I'd be cooler than that in the face of death. I always thought…wait.

You'd need ancient tech to hack it.

Ancient tech like the skeleton key I swallowed a hundred years ago. The little black orb that could take over anything back in my day. Manny notices it happen just as I do.

"Oh," he says, "yeah."

"As if I needed any more proof. You were never good enough for me," Hanah says.

"Maybe," I gurgle. "But I have more friends." "What?" Mary studies my face as the tunnel in my vision gets smaller and smaller. "Why are you smiling?" I'm smiling because as of about one half second ago, Manny is driving the robot.

Chapter 42

It might be the funniest thing I've ever seen.

All of the fragile future snakes who have caused so much pain and death and horror rush toward the gigantic copper robot, and Manny swipes them away in a single blow like they're matchstick men.

They fly like dandelion spores in the wind.

They break like china dolls on the walls.

They run. They scream. Most of them wet themselves and soil their robes and I cannot stop laughing.

Mary laughs with me.

Hanah screams and cries. And though I should definitely hate her, that's the one thing about this that isn't funny right now.

When the violence subsides and all of the snakes in the room are dead or dying, their stolen, harvested blood leaking onto the floor and our shoes, I march over to my wife as Mary closes and locks the vault door manually. No more serpents will be coming through here anytime soon.

"It's a trick," I demand. "Right? You're a hologram or you're a...clone or something? You're just in makeup or—"

"It's not a trick, Khalifa. It's just bad luck," Hanah says.

Mary starts looking for the secret tunnel that should lead to the secret spaceship to get us out of here. She's pulling on books on a shelf and hitting every button she can find. So far no luck.

"How? Why?" I'm screaming. My cool is well and truly lost and I think that's okay. I think I've earned that. "If you have enough resources," Hanah says coldly, "dying is a choice. Aging is a choice."

"The body farm," I say. "You just harvest new organs and blood and skin and whatever from the young."

"That's a simplistic way of looking at things. But you always were a simpleton. And this time you're not wholly incorrect."

I start pacing the room.

"But I saw your body. I saw you dead."

"You saw one of my parent's maids," she says calmly as if this weren't insane. As if she weren't unmaking my entire life right before my eyes. "She was hired because she looked like me. And when it was time for me to ascend to my throne, I needed to disappear in a way that would have people asking the fewest amount of questions. So she was dispatched and it was made to look like I was the one who died."

"But…" I say but stop. I can't finish the thought. It's too awful. So Hana finishes for me.

"Yes. That means that I was a part of this while we were married. And long before. And you never knew. I was recruited as a child, trained nearly from birth for this great and noble honour."

My heart races. My brain refuses to process it all. I think the rest of this conversation might actually kill me.

"If it's any comfort, I wanted to take you with me. I really did. Have you by my side as I guided the last age. But you were judged by the council and found…wanting." "I thought…I'm such an idiot. I actually thought you loved me."

Hanah actually seems vaguely human for the first time this century now. She softens just a little. "Because I did. I really did, Khalifa. Once. I just loved the future more." I swear.

A lot.

"You've killed so many people. You're one of history's greatest monsters, Hanah. How can that be even remotely possible?"

"Listen," she says, "I know it offends your stodgy little sensibilities, but a better future doesn't just happen on its own. Someone has to make it happen. And shaping history is bloody. Do you think Hitler was stopped with flowers and poetry? Or Genghis Khan? Or—"

"Stop! Just stop defending your horror show, lady."

"I do what has to be done to save our species, Khalifa." "You just kill random people by the thousands!" "No. It's not random. It's never been random. The people who die are all pieces of a vast machine that would take the world in dire directions. Sometimes they know they're part of the machine and sometimes they do not, but they are all cogs. Removing those cogs prevents disaster. They're cancers, husband. You don't coddle cancer cells. You burn them out of the body!"

"And how do you know—"

"We know. My organization has been doing this since before we counted time, Khalifa. We are the ones who got mankind out of the caves, we are the reason we lived while Neanderthals went extinct. Because we weeded the garden and shepherded the sheep. We are the ones who clawed humanity out of the dark ages and into the enlightenment. We are the people who curbed climate change. That alone saved literally billions of lives, Khalifa. I know you don't like it, I know you can't, but we are always the ones doing what needs to be done. Once, we used shamans and cunning men to understand the people who needed to be removed. Then philosophers and futurists. Now we have supercomputers that can identify threats long before they arise. I'm not a monster, Khalifa. I'm not a maniac. I'm a surgeon. I'm saving the whole world every single day." And then she actually has the lady balls to say, "You're welcome."

"You're nutty as a squirrel's cheeks is what you are, lady!" Mary shouts as she continues to search the room.

Then something occurs to me. Something terrible.

"And Humaid?"

"What about him?"

"Was his death faked, too? Is he still alive? Is he as horrible as his sister?"

She looks sad. Genuinely gutted. And I hate myself for it but it makes me happy.

"No. He was also lacking. And, like you, he wouldn't stop trying to find my killer. He was dogged and he was getting close. He, regrettably, had to be dealt with." "You killed your own brother for…for this?"

"I did what needed to be done. It's what I've always done, Khalifa. Look at what I've accomplished! Look at Dubai! It's safe! It's peaceful. It's perfect! The only violent crime in the city in decades was when you blew up a museum!"

"Oh it wasn't *that* violent," I say. Then, "But yes, let's look at Dubai! It was a shining jewel when we were born. Now…those people aren't even alive! They're just not dead yet. There's no spark. No humanity. Just fear and sadness and hopelessness. You've taken out all the artists and all the wild men and women who are dangerous and uncertain and who push us to great heights. You've done more than murder thousands of people, Hanah. You've killed the spirit of the world. You've neutered humanity."

"I preside over a utopia, Khalifa. It does not matter to me that you don't see it. And you cannot stop it. You can kill me if you have it in you to murder your wife. Maybe you can kill every single one of my servants on this moon. But there's no way off for you. Every ship is being fitted with explosives right now. Any attempt to leave and they all go up. It's over. You lost."

Hanah hits a button on her desk and a wall of monitors flips on. I see every ship on this moon, and they are all being wired to blow. Even the secret ship through the secret tunnel. It's no longer an option.

We're outnumbered basically a million to one with no way home.

We really are doomed.

We've left the future of the human race in the hands of insane killers.

I take a seat in my wife's chair and I don't have it in me to cry or scream or break things.

It's over.

We lost.

…

…

…

…

And then my radio crackles.

Chapter 43

I couldn't hear her voice at first, but only one person could be on this radio.

"Kha—" *kshhhh*.

She was more static than signal.

"Do you—" *ksnhhhnnn*.

She was too far out, still.

I held my breath.

And slowly, too slowly, she came in clearly.

"Khalifa." *Ksssshhh*. "Do you copy?"

I press the push-to-talk button so hard I almost break the radio. "I'm here, Afra."

I hear her laugh. "So is the cavalry," she says. "Look out the window."

"What's happening?" Mary asks.

"Yes," Hanah agrees for what will surely be the only time that happens. "What indeed, husband?"

I rush to the window to see nothing at first. Nothing but blackness and stars endless and growing.

Then.

A small ship appears. And then another. And then more.

A fleet of spacecraft comes into view one by one. I'm crying again. And laughing for the first time in a while.

Some are little spheres like the one we came in. Some are a little bigger, borrowed from private companies and air and space museums. Most are antiques like me.

They form a ring around the moon.

Like a halo.

"Wanna open the doors for us?" Afra asks.

"What have you done?" Hana demands. I ignore her.

"Manny. Can you let them into the hangar?"

"You're darn right I can," He says. And just like that, it's done. The moon welcomes a volunteer army here to save the future.

I guess it's Hanah's turn to laugh now. "Cackle" might be a better word. It's forced and it's hollow and it's mean, not unlike the world she's shaped while I was asleep.

"You're an idiot," she says. "You think you're the first would-be heroes to come here looking for blood? You think we didn't plan for an invasion? As soon as those people touch down, we'll activate the IDB bombs in their heads, just as we have every other time. Their skulls will explode in a rain of gore and horror. And, just like always, we'll be fine. We played the long game while you were on ice. I really thought you understood that we didn't just neuter your wild people that you're so fond of. We wired them to blow. We made sure from birth they couldn't hurt us. All you've done is slaughter a few hundred people and waste my time. That's it. No wonder they said you weren't worthy of me."

"She's right, Khalifa!" Mary says. "We can't let them land. Why didn't you run this by me? I could have told you. They'll die. They'll all die!"

"Because," I say, "They're already dead."

Everyone looks at me confused for a few beats. Manny gets it first and his laughter booms like shotguns of joy. Then Mary figures it out. "You clever son of a gun," she says. "You found the workaround."

Hanah is lost. She's spent her entire life in charge and in the know and at the other end of the guillotine. She doesn't like any of this.

"What?" She asks. "What does that mean?"

And on the wall of monitors, we watch the ships land one by one.

And we watch as none of their heads explode.

But the serpents fall by the droves.

They still have their swords, of course. And their poison. But it's no match for the guns and bombs and raw strength of my army of the dead.

"How?" Hanah demands. "How is this possible? What have you done!"

So I tell her about the crazy thing I asked of Afra that night when I blew up the museum.

I tell her how out in the desert were thousands of men and women like me. Relics tossed into the wishing well of time and forgotten. Frozen and alone and brave and angry like we used to be.

Wild.

Untamed.

Caring.

Fit.

Human.

And just waiting to be woken up.

I asked Afra to welcome them to the new world. I asked her to fill them in on what was happening. I asked her to see if anyone wanted to volunteer to save the world. Almost all of them raised their hands.

I asked her to do the one thing we both knew we could always do, even if I forgot for a while. I asked her to believe in the people of Dubai.

She used her police connections to feed them and to arm them and to borrow ships from all across the city and now they're here and now they're fighting back and now it's actually over.

Afra led them up here but stayed in orbit to avoid losing her head.

And it's really over.

We did it.

We won.

Her grandmother is so proud you can feel it from the afterlife. The barriers between life and death are no match for the joy of a great woman.

Some of the serpents scatter around the moon. Some retreat and hide and ambush. But they're no match for my kind. And soon enough they all surrender.

We have a hundred thousand years of proof of their crimes and an armada of ships to take it, and us, back home.

They'll be tried.

They'll be convicted.

Even Hanah.

I'll cry when they hang her by that perfect neck. But I won't regret a thing.

And the rest of us? We'll rebuild. We'll move forward.

For the first time literally in history, mankind will chart a path forward without this insane cult holding a poisoned knife to our throat.

It may be the first time since we walked out of the caves that we are truly free.

As we board one of the ancient ships headed back home Mary takes my hand and kisses me gently. "Do you think we can do it? Now that they're gone, do you really think we can make a finer world?" she asks. I smile and nod. "I do," I say. "We start at home and we will walk into a future that can actually be anything."

And I know we'll make it work.

I believe in the people of Dubai.

Ingram Content Group UK Ltd.
Milton Keynes UK
UKHW020644060723
424652UK00008B/194